THE SILVER CAYUSE

Big-framed, lean-faced Jim Tobey sometimes suspected he was nothing more than a fiddle-footed fool. Like the other boomers, he'd pulled up stakes and headed out California way on the gold trail, yet the yellow dust held no real lure for him. And he was only too glad to give up the search when a gun muzzle in the hands of a pretty girl pointed the way to a more dangerous adventure.

That land-hungry lobos should be trying to take possession of the vast Ranch of the Giants was understandable to Jim, and he knew how to take measures to curb them. But he couldn't savvy the hombres' interest in the girl's unusual silver cayuse ring.

THE SILVER CAYUSE

THE SILVER CAYUSE

by

LYNN WESTLAND

WILDSIDE PRESS

One

The creek, down below, was a bright thread of promise in the cradle of the hills. Jim Tobey, gaunt-faced, big-framed, his worn garments hanging loosely on him still, leaned against a tree and surveyed the scene with an eye which refused to kindle.

He had his strength back now, despite his gauntness, lingering mark of the cholera of the previous season. And this, he knew, was Mecca, the promised land. Here he was at last, and by rights he should be satisfied. But, as he had suspected a thousand miles back on the trail and a year before, he was a fool.

Just a fiddle-footed fool. Pulling up stakes back east, heading out this way on a trail of gold. For the most part, aside from his long sickness, he had enjoyed the trip from day to day, enjoyed the expectation of what might be over the next hill, around the next bend. And no one could dispute that the long trail of '49, or this hectic year of '50, had provided adventure enough along the way.

That was all well enough. So was this California country. A pretty country, in these green hills with the giant Sierras just behind them, frowning majesty in their hoary manes. Everything was as good as he had been led to expect, but what did it amount to?

What, when it came to that, did anything amount to? Jim Tobey shook his head. He vaguely understood now why, in days of old, a knight would spend his life in such a senseless-seeming quest as that of the grail. Probably he had never expected to find it, nor even seriously hoped. It had just given him something to do—for the knights must have been itching-footed fools like himself.

The trouble was that getting to new places didn't bring satisfaction with it. What was the sense in searching always for something if you could never find it? And how could you find it if you didn't even know what you were hunting for?

He shook himself impatiently. Ostensibly, he'd come all this long way, along with thousands of others, to find gold. But he'd been roaming the. country for weeks, with a hundred chances to stake a claim, and some of them good ones. There had been three places where he had dipped his pan and brought up more than color—nuggets which gleamed in the sun, and gave him a momentary thrill.

Others had staked those claims when he had neglected to do so. That didn't worry him. What was the use? Gold was good enough as an excuse. But gold wasn't what he wanted.

Well, he'd go down to the creek and get a drink. Good mountain water was better than whiskey, any day. He moved ahead and reached the creek, stepping out on a flat stone with the water gurgling around it. He was just starting to stoop down when the shot came.

The bullet pinged in the water just in front of him, with a curious effect. Jim Tobey saw how it happened. The bullet had struck the water itself first, with a little hollow gugrgle, but after going through a couple of inches of it, it slammed against the edge of the flat rock on which he stood, just below the water line, and knocked off a chunk, flinging it and a small geyser of water upward, almost into his face. Immediately after, from fifty feet upstream, just where brush grew in a rank clump, came the roar of the gun itself.

That was followed by the basso of a man's voice, harsh and short. Something like the coughing roar of a grizzly bear.

"Get back thar! Try jumpin' my claim and you get a grave on it!"

Jim Tobey turned, staring into the muzzle of the revolver, from which a thin whisp of smoke was ust starting to twist up. Behind it was a face framed in reddish whiskers, above a frame as big as his own and considerably beefier. Not a face to inspire confidence, at best. And right now it was twisted sourly.

"Jump!" the gunman repeated. "Out o' there before I kill you!"

Jim Tobey jumped, back to the shore. Anger was in him, but there was resignation along with it. This sort of thing was common enough these days—much too common, in fact.

"Don't get excited, feller," he drawled. "I don't hanker none for yore claim. Just aimed to get me a drink, was all."

The gun-muzzle did not waver, nod did the suspicion in the face behind it relax.

"Drink somewhere else, then! But travel out of here—pronto!"

Jim Tobey sighed, but he obeyed. It didn't pay to argue with guns. Nor even to get too mad at anybody who tried to crowd you. There were too many men, nerves frayed short by long bitter months on the trail, made tough and harsh by the things they had undergone, who were always trying to crowd everybody, as a matter of course. You couldn't fight the whole world—not with any profit or even much satisfaction. But the memory of the red-whiskered man remained in his mind as he went on, a little more unpleasantly than usual.

He secured his drink father down-stream, then paused to consider. The sensible thing to do, since he had lost all interest in staking a claim would probably be to head out for Sacramento or San Francisco. He'd looked those towns over, but there was always something new to see or do there, plenty of excitement—even a job, if that was what he wanted.

Irritably, he knew that he wanted neither the one nor the other. So, perversely, he turned and trudged back toward the higher, deeper hills. Back there, he had heard, no gold nor trace of it had been found. So it was still pretty primitive country. No place to go, viewed from a sensible standpoint.

"Mebby that's why I'm going," he decided. "According to most standards, I ain't got no sense, anyhow. Travel clear across the country, come clear out here to dig for gold—then too lazy to stake a claim!"

He shook his head at himself, partly in wonderment, more in amusement. Ordinarily, laughter came easily to Jim Tobey's lips. Lately there hadn't been much to laugh at. But a man could always laugh at himself, if he had any saving grace at all. If he couldn't do that, he was lacking somewhere.

And he wasn't lazy—not in the sense that he was afraid of work. It was just simply that gold, now that it was at hand, didn't interest him. Most people on the long trail would have been shocked to know that, in a belt around his waist, was more gold than most of them had ever seen. Or that, safely tucked in a bank, in case he ever wanted it, was plenty more—more than most of them had even dreamed of getting at the end of the trail.

He didn't look like a man with money, or act like it. But money, he had discovered, wasn't hard to make—at least not for him. One day, back East, his corn hoeing done, he'd sat down on the top rail of a fence and whittled a spell. And figured.

Then he'd built a model of the thing which had popped into his head, mostly just whittling it out. And later he'd got it patented. It had seemed like a fool thing to do. He'd known it probably wouldn't work, though the model had done all right. Even if it did, what would folks want of any contraption that he'd dreamed up? But a man liked to be doing something.

Strangely enough, folks had liked it. A man had seen it and wanted to buy it from him, and had paid him more than he'd ever dreamed of asking. Just like that. The trouble was, money wouldn't buy what you wanted. At least not for him.

He'd tried buying different things. Clothes. You couldn't walk far in tight new boots, or take half as much comfort in slicked up clothes as in old ones. Liquor. But water tasted better, any day. Left you feeling better the next morning, too. Trouble was, folks didn't appreciate water, since God had made it free. If it had to be made, like whiskey, and bought, they'd never think of drinking anything else.

Or food. You could buy that, fancy sorts. But he'd always had plenty in any case, and doing it up fancy didn't improve the taste. Fish eggs weren't half as good as corn bread and molasses. Or a trout, browned on a slab of bark.

Nope, after trying money out, he'd simply left most of it safe and jumped at the chance of doing what everybody else was doing, getting out to the gold country. That, with the cholera, had nearly killed him, and had kept him busy a spell, but it wasn't gold that he wanted. And now that he was here, he knew that he wasn't any closer to finding the thing he sought than he'd been back at the start.

"Reckon I'm a fool," he sighed. "How'n tunket can a man find somethin' when he don't even know what it is he wants?"

But that, he supposed, was what being fiddle-footed meant. You just kept on looking, because you couldn't find what you were looking for. And you couldn't find it because you didn't know what it was.

He ought to get himself a horse. Be easier, riding, back this way. Maybe he would, later.

That looked like a likely spot for trout. Deep

dark water, sent under the shadows of a grand-
daddy pine tree, with a little jerky waterfall just
above it. A couple of trout would go good for
supper.

They did. And the deep cushion of needles, on
the far side of the big tree, made as fine a bed as a
reasonable man could ask for. As he went on back,
the next few days, deeper into the still fastness of
the hills, where the leaves seemed to whisper a
secret that he was almost on the verge of catching,
Jim Tobey had a feeling that he was coming close
to what he sought for. That, at least, it was closer
here than it ever had been before.

He liked the remote solitude of this land, the
untouched grandeur of it. There had been spots
along the trail where he had felt the same thing,
in a lesser degree. Places like the Sweetwater, or
where the wild dash of Green River had suggested
a latent power and wildness that had nothing to do
with man. Or mountain crests where you could
look three ways—two of them down either side; or
else up, and seem near to climbing onto a star, lying
low there against the horizon.

Probably he might have found it at some of
those places if it hadn't been for the horde of gold-

seekers clogging the road, getting underfoot, obtruding on a man's thoughts, blanking out privacy. For three solid weeks he'd traveled in a line of wagons which in one respect was like God's mercy, seeming to have neither beginning nor end. Almost wheel to wheel for endless miles. And with dust like a fog above and around you, unending too.

This was something like it. No dust up here. No one to bother you. Here there was free, pure air to breathe, and room to breathe it in. He lost count of time, of the days as he simply wandered, a little farther back, a little deeper into the hills. Back here, he had a feeling he was the first man, like Adam. Or at least the first white man.

It was doubly jarring, just then when the belief had grown to conviction, and he was about to step across a creek which here was no wider than a good stride, to have a voice—and a woman's voice at that —halt him from a rocky thicket on the far side, while a gun muzzle poked a black snout at him.

"Stop, *Americano*, an' turn around—go back, before I keel you!"

Two

Jim Tobey blinked. It couldn't be true. Why, he hadn't seen a person, of any color or description, nor a sign of a settlement, for days. Yet the gun looked real enough, and now, looking more closely, he saw her there among the bushes, hidden by them like a grouse would be, blending just as well into them. A girl in a brownish dress, with brown hair that still caught the glint of the sun and seemed to set it rippling into gold, blue eyes and cheeks red with a sort of vivid excitement. And she wasn't holding the gun as if she knew how to use it.

"Sure, now, you wouldn't kill an innercent feller like me, would you?" Jim Tobey protested. "A purty gal like you. What you got it in for me for, anyhow?"

The girl looked a little startled and troubled at the same time. For she was only a girl, he saw now—she didn't appear to be more than twenty or so, at the most. And she reminded him of a startled rabbit, poised for flight, but curiously determined, just the same. Her breast rose and fell with her breathing, and he caught the glimpse of some trinket which she wore on a chain around her neck, hidden beneath her dress—something which flashed silver in the sun.

"Eet—eet ees not just you," she explained carefully, with a strange musical slurring of words which he couldn't quite figure out. "Eet ees—you are *Americano*, no?"

"Sure, I'm an American," Jim Tobey agreed. "You're one yourself, ain't you?"

She flushed, as if caught in a guilty secret, and half lowered the gun, which was an ancient sort of a musket, as he saw, then remembered and clutched it tightly again.

"I—I am sorry eef I am," she said. "Eet ees not my fault!"

"Not your fault! Good Lord!" Jim Tobey blinked. "Sure nothin' to be ashamed of, gal, bein' an American. Somethin' to be mighty proud of,

way it looks to me. That ain't what you meant,
I take it?"

"Well, eet—eet—" The blue eyes were peering
out at him, big and undecided and timid, like those
of a fawn. "Eet—it—that ees what I did mean, I
think. These Americano—they are mooch bad men,
yes?"

Jim Tobey scratched his chin thoughtfully.

"Well, you got somethin' there, I guess," he
conceded. "Some of 'em are pretty tough hombres,
for a fact. Don't know's I can blame you any for
bein' ready to meet 'em with a gun. But all Americans ain't that way. And how come you're sorry
for bein' an American? For I reckon that's what
you are, eh?"

"I—I guess I am," she agreed. "My parents, they
die when I am ver' tiny. And *Señor* Gonzales, he
warns me that the *Americanos* are ver' bad."

Jim Tobey settled himself comfortably on a
mossy rock on the far side of the little stream. He
did it very deliberately, fearful that a sudden movement might frighten her as it would a bird.

"And you were taken care of by this Mr. Gonzales, I take it?" he asked. "He's sort of looked
after you since you were a little shaver, eh?"

"But yes. And the *Señora*, of course. They have been ver' good to me. Now I try to help them."

"Why should they need help?" Jim queried interestedly. "Gettin' pretty old, are they?"

"They are old, yes. But eet ees not that. There ees the mooch trouble since the *Americanos* come to California. Most of our servant', they ron away for to dig the gold. The *Rancho el Gianto*, eet ees ver' big, and what can we do alone? And eef the *Americanos* come here—well, I try for to stop them," she added determinedly.

"And you figured I was aimin' to try and steal the ranch?" Jim Tobey demanded. "What's that mean—Ranch of the Giants, or somethin' like that? But you're wrong there. I ain't here to steal anything. Didn't even know there was a ranch in these parts. Though you ain't so far wrong in one way —there's plenty Americans would steal anything they could get hold of, and that's a fact. But I don't think there's any of 'em around this way to bother you. Leastways, I ain't seen sign of any. Still, the way you fooled me, there could be."

"Me? How did I fool you?" she asked. And he noticed that the gun had been lowered.

"Why, mostly just by bein' here. I thought I

was so far back in the hills, there wasn't anybody livin' around these parts, special nothing like a ranch—or anybody like you!"

"But you are now on the *rancho*," she explained. "And—you are here to try and find gold, ees that eet?"

Jim shook his head.

"Nope. Coulda found gold in other parts, I guess. Just wasn't int-rested in gold, seemed like."

She considered this, her piquant little face puzzled.

"But the *Señor*—he says that ees all that the *Americanos* want, ees—ees to find gold."

"I'm taking my hat off to the *Señor*," Jim agreed gravely. "Reckon he knows a heap about human nature—or what passes for that. But in my case I just wasn't int'rested. Just sort of wanted to get off by myse'f, back in the hills here, and kind of loaf, I guess. Been enjoyin' it more'n I ever thought a man could like anything. Must be a lazy streak in me croppin' out."

Again she considered this soberly for a while, then nodded understandingly.

"I know," she said. "I have feel the same way."

She flushed suddenly. "I theenk I say it wrong, no? Eet—it is so long since I have anyone to talk the *Americano* to, I am forget."

"You sure do it fine," Jim assured her. "Lot better'n I could do if I'd been talkin' Spanish or somethin' for a long spell, I bet. That's what you do talk, I suppose?"

"Oh, *si si.*"

Jim blinked.

"That some of it? Well, say—you ain't got no call to worry none about me. I'm Jim Tobey. Like I say, all I aim to do is sort of loaf around a spell, not botherin' nobody, and all I ask is to be let alone. Sure wouldn't want to cause no distress to you or the *Señor* or his wife. I hope you'll believe me."

"Why not?" she inquired with childlike faith. "You look like an honest man, *Señor* Jeem."

"*Señor* Jeem," he repeated. "Sounds kinda pretty, the way you say it. Never knew whether this homely mug o' mine looked honest or not. But I guess I am. Always aimed to be. What's your name —if you wouldn't mind telling me?"

"I am Jeanne," she said shyly. "Just Jeanne."

"Jeanne," he repeated. "That's a mighty pretty

name. Sort of fits you, too. How big a place is this Ranch of the Giants, anyway?"

"The *rancho?*" She puckered her brows thoughtfully. "Oh, eet—it is a beeg place—I am ride all the day over it, and still it is the *Rancho el Gianto*. Eet ees grant to the great-grandfather of the *Señor* by the King of Spain, I think."

"That way, eh?" Jim whistled. "Sounds like a big spread—and a good title. Which is a lucky thing, these days. Trouble is, why the folks are pourin' in from the East, there ain't much government these days, and titles don't amount to much. Don't know but what you folks are sensible, tryin' to take precautions."

Apparently she did not quite understand all of that. But, he reflected the next moment, there probably wasn't much of anything to worry about, way back in here. Nobody else was coming that far back in the hills. The latest strike news that he'd heard, before heading that way, had been off in a nearly opposite direction, and it had drained surplus men off after it like opening a spigot.

But for all that, he found himself vaguely uneasy, thinking of a big place, with two old people, deserted by most of their servants, and a pretty slip of a girl like Jeanne trying to guard its boundaries. Sure lucky it was so remote.

Apparently a new thought had just occurred to the girl, concerning the proprieties of talking thus to a man, and a stranger. She flushed painfully and started back.

"I mus' go," she said hurriedly. "You—you weel not bother any, then?"

Jim shook his head smilingly.

"Cross my heart an' hope to die," he promised. "I sure won't."

Her face relaxed a little.

"I remember, my father he used to say that, w'en I was ver' tiny," she said. "For long I have not remember. I theenk you are a good man, *Señor* Jeem. One to be trust.'"

"I sure hope I am," Jim agreed gravely. "I won't bother. Won't even trespass, if you'll tell me where to go to get back off the ranch. I hadn't aimed to bother."

"Oh, but you are only on the edge a little way," she assured him. "And eet—it is all right, since it is you. You—you are going to loaf some more, yes?"

"Yep, I reckon I'll just keep campin' back by that big mossy rock, by that waterfall, off upstream, a spell longer," Jim agreed. "If I won't be in the way. Sure like this country."

He saw the flash of that silver trinket which she wore as she moved again, light and graceful, shifting the heavy gun in her hand.

"That will be fine," Jeanne nodded. "I hope you have a good loaf, *Señor* Jeem."

She smiled rather timidly, then was gone with the same grace and suddenness of a fawn vanishing amid the underbrush. Jim stared after her for a moment, almost inclined to rub his eyes and wonder if he had dreamed the whole thing or not. It was unbelievable. But she had been real enough. Utterly unlike any person he had ever met before—and somehow a lot more to his liking than most girls, despite, or maybe because of that.

Not that he had ever had much to do with girls. Usually they frightened and bewildered him, strange, unpredictable creatures. Jeanne was shy, but he had liked her. He wondered if he'd ever see her again, and decided that it was unlikely. And he couldn't go looking for her.

Strangely he could not get her out of his mind. Not even after he had returned to his little impromptu camp by the waterfall, and made a satisfying meal of a snared grouse roasted in hot coals, after being wrapped in a coating of clay. With succulent strawberries, wild and red and juicy and sweet as remembered dreams, for dessert. He was still thinking of her when he dropped off to sleep, and it seemed to him that it must be all a part of the dream when he heard her voice calling him and sat up, to find her bending above him, shaking him with fierce, urgent hands, her excited breath warm on his face.

"*Señor* Jeem!" she implored. "Oh, Jeem—wake up! They 'ave come—the bad ones! I must have help! *Señor* Jeem!"

Three

Wide awake now, Jim sat up, tossing back his blanket. Jeanne was real enough, and the apprehension in her voice was an urgent thing. He reached for his boots.

"What is it, Jeanne?" he asked. "What's the trouble?"

"Oh, eet—is is the *Americanos*, I theenk, *Señor* Jeem. They come, just before it grows dark—many of them, with gons, and they are bad. I think they rob and steal. And what happens now, I do not know! I know we must have help, and so I theenk of you, that you will be here by the waterfall. I come. You will help me?"

"You bet I'll help you," Jim agreed, standing up. "Lead the way."

She did so, promptly. After a moment, for it

was very dark in there beneath the big trees, her hand stole out to his to guide him.

"I brought horses," she explained. "You can ride?"

"Guess I can ride 'most anything, if I have to," Jim conceded. "Always been pretty good that - way."

In a little open glade, where the faint thin light of the moon came through, two saddled ponies waited, and his eyes glinted at sight of them. Here were blooded stock—no plains cayuses, but blood of old Spain, crossed with the best of the wiry survivors of others of that ancient line. They had big Spanish saddles, ornate with the trappings of Mexico and California, and as he swung into one of them, Jeanne was up, and he saw that she rode as naturally as she breathed. They had gone a little way when she turned to him, her voice breathless.

"Am I do wrong?" she asked him. "I can theenk only of you for to help, Señor Jeem—and you too are an Americano. But you are not like those other men—you weel help?"

"You bet I'll help," Jim repeated. "And you did just right. Now how many of them are there? And how many men has the Señor got to back him?"

"I theenk there were four, maybe five," she said gravely. "All with gons. They come so suddenly—eet—it is like the bad dream. For us, there is the *Señor*, who is brave like the lion, and the *Señora*, of course. There there is Pedro, and Margarita, the cook. And Tony, from the stables, who limps. But Pedro is old, and Margarita can only cook—"

She ended on a small note, almost of despair. Jim's mouth tightened. He could pretty well picture it already. He wished that he had a gun; one of those new six-shooters would help a lot in a case like this. He'd never really felt the need for a gun before, though he'd used a rifle on guard duty and in a skirmish or so with the Indians. But for himself, he'd always felt that a man could do better without a gun. Packing one lent you a false sense of superiority, and had a way of getting you into trouble, trouble which wasn't apt to come your way if you didn't pack the open invitation to it.

Tonight was different. Though he had supposed that he was too far back in the hills to be near any settlers, here was the Ranch of the Giants. Here, too, had come a motley rabble, out for trouble. Prospectors, probably, who had strayed that way and discovered the lonely ranch instead of gold, and had been quick to note its unprotected state.

The fact that they were turning their hand to robbery proved them to be rabble. It was an ironic commentary on life, but true, that the rough and ruthless, the mean, low-down sort who were frowned upon in any decent community, had made the trip across the continent in far larger numbers proportionately than the hard-working and decent.

They had traveled three or four miles, going at a steady trot, when Jeanne slowed her horse and turned to him. Ahead of them loomed a dark huddle of buildings, and a single light shone like a dim beacon.

"I do not know what to do," Jeanne confessed. "But here we are."

"Let's have a look before we go bustin' in," Jim suggested. "May be able to do a lot more good that way."

They left their horses, and went ahead on foot. Even in the dark, he could see that this had once been a great estate, and probably still was, though already there were signs of neglect.

That was one of the curses of the gold rush. He had seen plenty of farms, mighty nice ones, left to wither as from a blight. Whatever the gold meant to the pouring tide of forty-niners, their coming was completely overturning the mode of life of those who had held this land.

He saw that there were many buildings there. A great, sprawling house which had been a sort of feudal castle right up to the present, big barns, corrals. It was different from anything he had ever known, yet curiously like his boyhood home in some respects. And then a voice from the gloom ahead cut harshly through the night, ripping across his thoughts.

"Get a rope over that tree-limb, Bart. Now then, feller, the jig's up. We got this place—and we're takin' over. But we want to know where that gal is. Tell us mighty quick, or we'll let you dance a jig—on air!"

They were leading the *Señor* out—Jim could tell that, not only by the quick indrawn gasp of the girl beside him, and her convulsive clutch on his arm, but by the look of the man who was shoved roughly ahead of the others now came into a patch of brighter moonlight beside a great tree.

He was a tall man, the *Señor* Gonzales, dressed in the California fashion, with a sort of rich but quiet elegance. His hair was gray, and he carried his head high, despite the fact that there was a smear of blood down his right temple, that his jacket had been half ripped from him, and that his hands were tied behind his back.

Behind him, shoved along as unceremoniously, Jim could see the others—a little old lady in a Spanish shawl who he knew must be the *Señora* and old Pedro, who walked as though dazed from a blow. Margarita, who was so fat that she could barely waddle, her eyes streaming helpless tears of rage and frustration. And Tony, the stable-boy, limping, with a dull, hopeless look on his face. All of them with their hands tied.

But it was the leader, the man who had issued the order, who caught Jim's instant attention. Here was one of those meetings which the books would call coincidence, but which, Jim had long since discovered, a sly fate has a way of arranging. This was the red-whiskered man who had ordered Jim off his claim a week or ten days before, when he had been about to get a drink. How had he happened to leave it and come here, with this pack of rats at heel?

For that was as good a description of them as

any, Jim saw. There were four of them, men to match their boss. One was a big man, slouching, who walked with a limp, and who had a smiling face the more terrible because of that. Two were small, and yellow-haired, and so alike that they must be twins. Men not over five feet five in their boots, and with viciousness stamped on their faces. The other man was ordinary enough, with nothing to set him apart in any company.

They halted their prisoners, checking the *Señor* with a rough jerk. The coppery whiskers on the leader's face had gone untrimmed since their last encounter, Jim saw; his eyes held a reddish glint to match.

"How about it?" he growled. "Yuh ready to talk?"

Gonzales' only answer was a shake of the head. Jeanne's fingers bored into Jim's arm.

"But he cannot talk the *Americano*," she whispered. "Oh, what can we do?"

"Take it easy," Jim cautioned. "They think they've got everything their own way, and they're in no hurry. We'll watch for a chance."

He knew that the element of surprise would be all in their favor when he was ready to make a move. Since they probably had kept a watch on the place for a while before making their attack, this gang knew that they had taken everyone captive with the exception of Jeanne, and they were not worried about what she might be able to do.

But when he did act, he needed to make it count. For if he made a slip, and even one of the five got away in the dark, with a gun, it would be a touch and go proposition from then on. It was no time to make mistakes.

Red-whiskers carried a rifle. It looked like a Mississippi rifle to Jim, and was easily the best weapon there, aside from a Colt's six-gun which the leader also carried. The rifle was a percussion gun, and it was of course loaded and ready for use. If he could only get his hands on it—

And it looked as though he might. For now it was being stood up against a smaller tree.

"Tell you how it is, Pop," the leader intoned now, spitting on his hands and swinging a rope ominously. "This looks like a right nice place yuh got here—and we're takin' over. Californy belongs to Americans now. So this'll be ours now. Easiest way is for us to hang all of you an' be done with it. But if you'll talk up an' tell us where that gal's hidin', we'll let yuh go with yore lives. And yuh got Hank Donney's word for that!"

Apparently that promise was not a reassuring one. There was no answer, no sign on the part of Gonzales that he had heard at all. Jim had almost reached the rifle.

"Dang it, don't any of yuh understand English?" Donney barked. "Must be some way of talkin' to 'em!"

"The old un, there, he knows it. I know that," the man who had seemed not to belong spoke up suddenly.

"Yuh shore of that, Jeb? Then, Pop, yuh better talk—and quick! How about it? Be easier than dancin' on air!"

Jim reached, his fingers closed on the barrel of the rifle. A scheme was building in his head. And there was nothing like a scheme when something needed doing.

Four

With the rifle in his hands, Jim Tobey edged back to where he could watch them all, then whispered his instruction to Jeanne. She hesitated only a moment, looking into his face, and then, steadily, with a fine high courage, she walked out into the moonlight. She called something to the captives in Spanish as she came.

Her sudden appearance produced the effect that Jim had counted on. All attention was centered on her, and Donney was starting toward her, all else forgotten, when Jim's voice halted them in their tracks.

"Anybody that makes a move, dies," he warned. "Lift your hands, and keep 'em high!"

There was a moment of hesitation, of appalled indecision. But now they could catch a shadowy glimpse of him, and see the rifle more clearly, its barrel leveled and covering them. While they were still hesitant, Jeanne carried out the rest of his instructions. She moved quickly, slipping around behind Donney, and had snatched the revolver from his holster before he quite realized what was happening.

The rest was simple enough—disarming and tying them, then freeing their captives. There were exclamations, and a little weeping, and much excited talk, but through it all, Jim saw to it that the five were herded away and locked, separately, in rooms from which escape would be pretty well out of the question. There were such rooms in that old half feudal ranch house.

The look of mingled recognition, rage and incredulity which Hank Donney gave him would have stirred apprehension in most men. Curiously enough, it gave Jim a lift.

"This sort of evens things up," he said. "You should've stayed with that claim you was so fond of."

"Wan't no gold on the danged thing," Donney said disgustedly. "But talkin' of evenin' up—there'll be more of that, later!"

"Shouldn't be surprised," Jim agreed. "Looks

to me like there's room for it—and room to string
the bunch of you up on that big tree, come mornin'."

He was introduced to the others, to the Gonzales, to Pedro and Tony and Margarita. She had
to make some sort of an explanation as to where
she had found him when help was so urgently
needed, and how she had known of him; and watching her, seeing the color rush across her face, Jim
knew that she was telling the simple truth.

Her judgment had been vindicated, and there-
fore there was no blame for her. The fact that they
all had to talk through Jeanne as interpreter made
little difference. He was an *Americano*, but they
welcomed him with the warm hospitality of a
warm-hearted people, and with the affection due
a deliverer. Jim felt a little diffident. He hadn't
done much of anything.

And the thing which they seemed to overlook,
but with kept crowding into the niches of a prac-
tical Yankee mind, was what could be done now.
They had been in the depths of a bottomless de-
spond a little while before. Now they were lifted
to the heights. Everything was going to be all right.

He wished that he could share a little of that

simple faith. But the more he looked at the ranch, even in the night, and listened to things, the worse it seemed. For a while now, things had pretty much run themselves, so far as he could judge.

Which meant that the cattle had strayed where they pleased, without let or hindrance. Most of the original herds were probably still somewhere on the broad acres of the original King's grant. Other things had been left to take care of themselves too, while the crew which had once looked after them delved in strange, far places for the metal which puts a fever in the blood and a madness in the minds of men.

So far, it hadn't mattered too much. There had been plenty of grass, and enough momentum from the past to keep things going, after a fashion. But that momentum was about used up now, so that it was creaking to a stop like a bogged-down Conestoga in a mud hole. And there was change in that land of California—change with a capital D for disaster.

Even with Donney and his men captured, and barring the probability that there would be more of their same ilk along later, how was the ranch to be run, without a crew? This was California's country—but it was utterly unlike the soft, rich land which he had seen before. Up there in the mountains, there were signs of fall already. It would soon be winter, with snow—much snow.

It looked like a good place for a ranch, and a wonderful place to live. Under the proper conditions, which included things as they had been, with a big crew to do the work, loyally, uncomplainingly, and with nothing different or better to look forward to, no other change of occupation possible.

Now, without a crew, how would the cattle, the ranch itself, survive the winter? Winter meant work—feeding of hay which had not even been cut during this profligate summer, herding of cattle grown wild during the days of freedom. That and much more.

The more he considered it, learning a little here, a little there, by a casual question or so, the more worried Jim Tobey grew. These people, the Gonzales, with their few faithful, completely ineffectual servants who had remained with them—they were like children in a forest. Lost and bewildered. Babes in the wood, quite literally. Gonzales had been able to cope with life as he knew it, in the place where he had been born and had fitted by tradition.

That was as a word of the manor, with servants at his beck and call. Now he was too old to change, to realize what change meant. Jeanne alone was young and fresh and vigorous, and he saw a little of his own uneasiness reflected in her face.

He wanted quite desperately to shake off responsibility, to go back to his big tree by the waterfall, to the life which had been his only a few hours before. He had come to the rescue when asked to do so, and now his part should have been ended. After all, what were they to him? But he knew, even while he fought against it, that this was something that he had to take the responsibility for, like it or not. Chiefly because of a pair of bright, trusting eyes, which looked to him now with such faith and hope.

And he knew that he wasn't going to mind the responsibility, or the size of the job. Not under those conditions.

Only how was he going to do it? That was the appalling part. He couldn't let them down—but how could he do anything else? Here was a job for a giant, and he was no slayer of dragons.

They talked for a little while, and had something to eat, and then, finally, after he had made another round to make sure that the prisoners were secure, with Tony on guard, he was shown to a room which made him blink unbelievingly, and left to sleep.

"And I guess I need it," he muttered. "Tomorrow we'll see how things look. Can't look no worse than they do now."

Yet, curiously enough, he wasn't worried about it as he went to sleep. He felt more contentment than at any time since he'd decided to follow the trail of the forty-niners. He had something to do— something that he rather wanted to do.

Morning brought him back to reality. He knew, on awakening, that he'd been dreaming, and that it had been a pleasant dream. Jeanne had been somewhere in it. The details were hazy, but that part was easy to remember. Now, however, there were things to do, decisions to be made. The first of these was what to do with their captives.

He discovered that the solution, in the mind of the *Señor*, was perfectly simple. They would simply take them out, all five, and kill them. The method was the only thing to puzzle over. They deserved hanging, but it would involve a chore.

Shooting them with a pistol would probably be simpler. The hand of Gonzales was still perfectly steady for such a task, and he had hit upon an expedient which would remove most of the trouble, that of burying them afterward.

They would be made to dig their own grave first—one big one, into which all five could be tumbled. Pedro and Bart could fill it in without too much trouble. Since the five had been engaged in open banditry, with threat of murder, and had been caught in the act, there was, to the mind of the old rancher, no question of justice or ethics involved.

Likewise, these five were *Americanos*—heathens by that very token, so it was not necessary to worry about a burial service.

Jim Tobey wished that he could accept the simplicity of this. It was undoubtedly the best way out of a bad situation—if only the one aspect was considered. And it was what he had suggested to the five would happen to them, but that had been to give them bad dreams, not meant seriously.

Yet if the five were left alive, they would be vengeful and up to more mischief, unless taken out to the law—when and if law could be found—convicted and dealt with my it. That would be a big chore, a risky one, and an uncertain sort of thing in an uncertain land. But it would have to be done that way.

"We can't just kill them, *Señor,*" he explained.

"This isn't the California of the old days. You were pretty much the boss here then, I guess. If you decided to kill a few bandits, nobody would say a word. But you had the government of Mexico behind you then, as well as your neighbors and a big crew. Now you haven't got any of them."

Señor Gonzales listened politely while Jeanne explained this, but he looked puzzled.

"But they deserve to die," he said simply, with irrefutable logic.

"Sure they do," Jim agreed. "But there's a law in this country—when there is any law. And five men are just too many to kill and have disappear. There'd be sure to be trouble, sooner or later. They'll have friends somewhere—even their kind do. First thing we know, the law would be after us for murder. It just won't do."

It was beyond his powers of explanation, or those of Jeanne, to make this clear. If he said it was so, Gonzales was willing to take his word for it. After all, had he not been their savior in time of

direst need? But such a law was the great foolishness, which did not make sense. And if they didn't
kill them, what would they do with them?

He was the perfect host, but it was plain that his
already poor opinion of *Americanos* in general had
been strengthened. He made no exception of Jim.
As to the law, Jim was inclined to agree with him
on that, but it didn't alter things. And then, while
he was trying to think how to explain it all more
logically, Jeanne turned from the window excitedly.

"Others come," she said. "More *Americanos*,
too!"

Five

The feel of the six-shooter strapped about his waist was a comforting thing in that moment. This man Colt had made a good invention when he'd worked out a gun that would shoot six times. There weren't many of them in the country yet, and it gave a man a big advantage when he had one of them. Right then, Jim felt that he needed all the odds he could get.

He'd been afraid, for no very good reason, of some such development. Trouble usually went in strings. But, looking out the window, he was puzzled and partially reassured. There were four this time—men on horseback, riding up quite casually, and Americans, all right. But his first guess that they would be friends or confederates of Donney seemed a little wide of the mark as he looked at them more closely.

Three of them might have been anything. There was nothing to set them apart from the common run of humanity, either in the clothes they wore or the looks on their faces

But the fourth man, so far as clothes and manner went, and face too, was a gentleman. Jim Tobey had seen his like, back in Vermont and down Boston way. Clean-shaven, except for glossy sideburns that had seen a comb no longer ago than the morning. A long, thin face, and the clothes that a banker or trader would wear. There were a few such men in Sacramento and San Jose and San Francisco, for the Yankee strain had a way of poking its inquisitive and acquisititive nose into every corner of the globe, especially when something of more than passing interest was going on. Somehow it wasn't strange to see him there now.

He was dismounting casually, and the others were following his example. He stopped and cast a sharp look at Tony as he hurried up to take their horses, and what might have been behind the look no man could guess. But when Gonzales appeared in the doorway of his house and stood there, a straight, dignified figure, the other man advanced courteously.

Though he certainly didn't look the part to be included in such fine company, with his boots down at heel and that six-shooter strapped about his middle, Jim Tobey figured that he'd better be in on this, so he came to stand beside the *señor*.

The four, it appeared, were simply having a look at the country. A little more than that, too, as Gregory Collier confessed, after having introduced himself and been invited inside. He was quite newly arrived in the California country, having come by sea, across the isthmus and up to San Francisco. Lured by the fabulous stories of gold, of course.

But, quite frankly, he wasn't so much interested in gold, now that he was there. His interest ran more to the big ranches, and he had heard of the Ranch of the Giants, and had been frankly curious to have a look at it. Even, if it was for sale, to consider the possiblity of purchasing it.

It was a perfectly reasonable story, told in a straightforward manner, and Jim Tobey was not just sure why he found himself disbelieving it. *Señor* Gonzales, he saw, had no doubts. It had always been his custom to accept a gentleman at face value, and this man, though an *Americano*, was quite obviously a gentleman.

Only one idea startled the *Señor*. The notion of selling *El Gianto*—that had never entered his head. Yet now the seed had found lodgement in a fertile spot. Things being as they were, it might be the simplest way out of a bad situation. He would give the matter consideration.

Margarita served refreshments, and they chatted amiably, while his men wandered about outside, one of them whistling cheerfully. Collier asked Jim a few questions about himself, in an amiable and condescending manner. He assured his host that he wanted him to take plenty of time to consider the idea before making up his mind. He even wanted more time to look over the ranch himself, though the more he saw of it, the more pleased he was with the whole notion of acquiring such an earthly paradise.

The talk inevitably came to the visitors of the night, and the fact that they were prisoners now. Jim, watching closely, could detect only a natural interest in Collier's face or voice at this recital. He agreed with the *Señor's* expressed opinion that they deserved to be shot, but he backed Jim's stand that it simply wouldn't do—not in view of the new order which had come to California.

"There's a new law—where there is any law," he commented. "And, as our friend Jim points out, that law sooner or later would probably get around to asking questions, and they would regard your action as high-handed, to say the least."

He sipped his coffee thoughtfully a long moment.

"But I can appreciate your predicament. You are short-handed now, and these thugs are not easy to dispose of. If you'll allow me, I have a suggestion. I am rather well known to the authorities in this country—in fact, I have the personal acquaintance of Governor Burnett. He is, I may add, a fine, high-minded type of gentleman.

"He will probably be at San Jose, and it's only a matter of a couple of days of steady riding to reach there, where the real law of the state is. Since we'll be riding in that general direction again today, we will, if you like, take these five off your hands. I assure you that they will be taken to the proper authorities, and dealt with as they deserve. I will personally see to that. Of course, it's only a suggestion."

But it was a good one, a very good one, the *Señor* assured him, hugely relieved. If it would not be imposing too much on his good nature, his generosity, to so burden him with such a company of riffraff—

It would be no trouble, Collier repeated. A pleasure, indeed. For since he was interested in making California his own home, he was doubly interested in bringing about a restoration of law and order.

It sounded like a good solution, and Jim Tobey offered no adverse comment. But his own suspicions weren't entirely lulled. Collier was a gentleman, of that there could be no question. But there had been a gambler, way back in Nebraska, who certainly knew how to behave like a gentleman—until a rough and ready court had lynched him just as the Laramie was in sight, for proven crimes which were no less savage for having been done in a gentlemanly way.

The prisoners were brought out, and Jim, watching closely, had to confess that he could see no sign of recognition between them and the newcomers. But those other three had been prowling around outside—and come to think of it, all three of them had whistled, and all had chosen the same tune, at intervals. Of course, it was a popular tune—"Oh

Susannah." It might mean nothing. But it could have been a signal.

"I'll see to it that they are taken to the law, and given the full penalty for what they deserve," Collier promised, as the five were made to mount horses, their hands again tied behind their backs. "When I return—which I hope to do in a week or ten days—I'll probably be able to report that American justice can be as swift and sure as your own, *Señor* Gonzales. Meanwhile, let me assure you that you will have nothing more to fear from them."

He swung to his own horse, riding the skittish animal with practiced ease, lifted his hat gallantly, then they were off, heading down the one road which lead out to the valleys. Having discovered that Tony could understand some English, and having already given him his instructions, Jim lost no time in suggesting a ride to Jeanne.

She looked at him, a little surprised, but, seeing the look on his face, agreed. Before the others were out of sight, they were riding off in an opposite direction.

Two minutes later, back among the trees, they encountered Tony, and Jim explained.

"I'm going to circle around through the brush

and keep an eye on those fellows for a while. You and Tony ride up the hill there, along that trail. If they look back, they'll be able to see you—and they'll think I'm still with you."

Jeanne's face was a little troubled.

"You—you do not trust them?" she asked.

"It's just as well to be sure of what we can," Jim said briefly. "I'll be back later. Don't say anything to the others, either of you."

Jeanne nodded soberly, and Jim swung off through the trees, riding fast, making a big circle. This Ranch of the Giants was literally that, he knew now, and it would take a long time and a lot of riding to get familiar with the general lay of the land. But for the moment, he knew where he wanted to go, and how to get there.

He came out, half an hour later, at a point two miles farther down the road. By taking a short cut, where the road made a big bend, he knew that he had gotten ahead of the others. And by this time they would be sure that they were well out of ear and eye of any of the handful who remained on the ranch. If they had entertained any doubts, they could look and see the only two who were young and vigorous enough to follow, apparently climbing a trail high up the mountainside.

Jim saw the two, too far off to recognize. He placed his own horse back out of sight as the sound of others reached his ears, and for a few moments, seeing the prisoners still riding, tied securely, he wondered if he had misjudged the man. Then, not a hundred feet away from where he watched, he saw Collier pull his own horse to a stop. His voice was sardonic.

"I guess you boys have ridden that way far enough, and it's probably as uncomfortable as it looks," he commented. "Untie them, before we go on."

Donney's face contorted savagely.

"And then we go back and clean up on them," he growled. "That it, eh, boss?"

Six

Collier shook his head decisively.

"No," he said. "I don't war on women."

"You mean, you're givin' up grabbin' that ranch?" Donney demanded incredulously, flexing his cramped arms.

Collier smiled, a tight, mirthless gesture.

"There's more than one way of skinning a cat," he reminded Donney softly. "I had expected you boys to have the job done, and the situation under control. My bold, bad men!"

"Things didn't go right," Donney complained. Seated there in the saddle, he looked ugly, but still curiously like a small boy about to burst into tears. "He even took my gun. Ain't we going to get that back?"

"Maybe he'd object to giving it back," Collier said softly. "No, I think we'll just consider that as

donated to the good of the cause. We won't disturb them for a while—and not so crudely another
time, in any case. I shall handle this myself."

With which pronouncement he led the way on
down the road. Jim Tobey watched them go with
mingled feelings. This was pretty much as he had
expected, except that Collier was a more dangerous
man than had seemed apparent at first. Just what
he was up to, there was no sure way of telling. But
that made it all the worse.

Jim made his own way back, viewing things
now with an appraising eye. The ranch was showing signs of neglect; the hay fields were uncut, and
a lot of things needed to be done. But it was still
in good shape, and his eye kindled at a number of
haystacks, carried over from the year before. If
part of this hay could be harvested, there would be
enough to winter a considerable herd of cattle,
despite everything. Provided the ranch could be
kept going at all.

There was the rub. It was impossible to run
much longer without a good crew, and gathering
them would not be easy, in times such as these. If
trouble came, a crew was needed to defend the
ranch against men like Donney. And the fall round-

up and branding would soon have to be taken care of.

He caught himself, and smiled a little wryly. Here he was planning as though he were responsible for everything. But wasn't he? Unless he did it, it wouldn't be done. That was a certainty. And with Collier laying plans for getting possession of the ranch, it was up to him. You couldn't quit in the middle of a job of that sort.

Circling, he met Jeanne before she had returned to the house, finding her warmly excited about all that had been happening, eager for his report. She listened gravely, her face troubled.

"Oh, Jeem," she said. "What would we do weethout you? You will stay and help us, won't you?"

"Of course, if you want me to," he agreed. "Though whether I'll be much good or not remains to be seen."

"I think you're fine," she said so sincerely that he felt a little uncomfortable, and far prouder than he had any right to feel. Maybe *Señor* Gonzales wouldn't want him bothering in the affairs of the ranch, he added.

But Jeanne was very certain that the *Señor* would

want him to help. Which proved to be the case. Gonzales was shocked that a man could appear to be so fine and straightforward a gentleman as Collier had seemed, and still be a knave. But he was pathetically helpless. This new day and age, he confessed, was beyond his understanding. If only they could return to the simple, untroubled life which he had known before, rather than these world-shaking times of change!

The first thing, Jim decided, was to get a crew. That would mean going where men were. After that, he wasn't just sure. It meant leaving the ranch for a few days, and he didn't like that—not with Jeanne staying behind. But it had to be done. And he realized that there would be less risk now than later. Whatever plan Collier had in mind, it had to do with indirection rather than force, and there would probably be a lull of days, perhaps weeks, before he was ready to take new steps.

Gonzales showed a readier grasp of the situation than Jim had expected. He pointed out that they were dependent now on Jim, who was a stranger, but who had helped 'them once, and so they were resolved to trust him. And that, accordingly, it was up to Jim, if he would be so kind, to act as foreman, which would give him the necessary authority along with the responsibility.

The dignity with which this confession was made was a little pathetic.

"I am helpless, and I know it, in a time such as this," Gonzales said sadly. "In any case, my day is done. My heart, it bothers me, these days. I cannot work as I once did, or as I would. Not much of anything at all."

"I'll do my best," Jim promised. "How good that'll be, no tellin'. But I won't let you down for lack of tryin'."

He prepared to start the next morning, with one of the best horses on the ranch to ride, a tireless animal which could go for hours or days at a good clip if need be. Gonzales said proudly that he believed the horses on the Giant to be the finest stock in California. And Jim had to grant that he had something to boast of.

Evening should bring him back to the low country, to the diggings, and there he hoped to find disillusioned men who, having spent their all to get to the land of gold and finding nothing, would be hard up and eager to take a good job for a while, to accumulate a fresh grubstake.

It would mean hiring his fellow-countrymen, of course, rather than the Mexicans and Californios who had always made up the crew of the ranch. But since he had to talk to them, that would be an advantage. The thing now was to get them.

He was saddling his horse when Jeanne came out to the barn.

"You are going now, Jeem?" she asked, and, quite suddenly, Jim Tobey knew why it was that he had been dreading the trip today. He didn't like to go away and leave her behind.

"Guess I sort of have to dust along," he agreed, tugging at the cinch. "Sooner I go, sooner I can get back."

"I weel be glad when you return," she assured him. "Oh, Jeem—I am afraid. Where you go, there is so much danger. You weel be careful?"

"I'll sure do my best that way," he said. "But I don't think there'll be much risk for me. It's you folks that I'm kinda worried about."

"We weel be careful," she promised. "But you —I have something for you, Jeem. Here."

Flushing a little, she reached inside her bodice and pulled out the silver chain which he had noticed before. At the end of it was the object whose gleam he had once seen—a man's ring, embossed, curiously wrought and carved. It seemed to be of heavy solid silver. It was still warm from her touch as she tendered it.

"I think this will maybe fit on your beeg finger, eh?" she asked, and, breathing a little faster, slipped it on the first finger of his right hand. "There, it does fit you!" she exclaimed triumphantly, slipping it off the chain.

Jim looked at it curiously, then with a quickening interest. The design, he saw, was that of a rearing horse—a strong, wiry range cayuse, very lifelike. It was an excellent job on the part of the silversmith.

"Eet—it is good luck, the silver cayuse, to who wears it," Jeanne explained. "So I want you to take it, please. You weel need good luck, I think."

She slipped the chain around his own throat, then stood back, laughing a little.

"For years—since I can remember—I have carried this," she said. "But it is a man's ring, and not for a lettle finger like I have. You it fits so well."

"It does fit pretty well," Jim admitted. "But—but I don't want to take this, Jeanne. It belongs to you. A sort of a keepsake, I reckon, ain't it?"

She nodded, her face sobering a little.

"Yes. I think it belongs probably to my papa—eet is all I have that my parents ever had. But that eet—it is good luck, I have been told. So you weel wear it."

"I'll take it along on this trip, if you want me to, and I'll sure be careful of it," Jim agreed, more touched than he cared to admit. "But what do you know about your folks, Jeanne?"

She shook her head doubtfully.

"Almost nothing. They were *Americano*—and something happened to them when I was small. Whether it was Indians, or the desert, or the hard-sheeps—all that I know is what leetle the *Señor* has been able to tell me. They took me, he and the *Señora*, to raise me, a leetle lost waif. To them I have been as a daughter, always. They tell me that the ranch, it will be mine, and all that belongs to it. They have been very good to me—even if I am the *Americano*, the gringo."

"They've never liked Americans, have they? And I can't say that I blame them much, everything considered."

"No. But me they raise, just the same. I remember only a little—my father, I think, a man with a stern face, but kind. My mother, holding me close in her arms, as if to protect me—from what seems like a bad dream then. But it is mostly forgotten. All that I remember to tell was my name, Jeanne. God—and the Gonzales—have been very good to me."

"I imagine they feel that God has been very good to them, too, sending you to them," Jim declared. "I think I've been caught up in that luck, strayin' this way. Guess I been lookin' for this place—and you—all my life, without ever knowin' what it was I wanted."

He stopped, suddenly self-conscious, surprised that he could think or say such things. He smiled suddenly, and swung to the saddle.

"With this luck, and you waitin' here for me, I'll sure get things done," he agreed. "I'll be back in a few days. So long, Jeanne!"

She was still watching him when he reached the turn of the road. Waiting. Sombody to come home to!

Seven

Jim Tobey studied the ring as he rode, turning it on his finger. It was apparently the only tangible link with Jeanne's past, and it was supposed to represent good luck. Or so she believed.

The rearing cayuse stood out boldly from the rest of the ring, lifelike. But the ring was a trifle loose on his finger, and he slipped it off again, back onto the chain. He'd carry it, but he'd take good care that nothing happened to it.

It was his intention to get a crew hired as speedily as possible and to get back to the ranch with them. But if he could keep an eye on Collier and his movements during the same journey, that would be all to the good. He had a feeling that there was more behind Collier's visit than had yet been revealed—that something big had lured him there in the first place. The Ranch of the Giants was so far

off the beaten track that the thing could hardly be
a coincidence.

Collier had apparently figured on stealing the
ranch itself, through his hired thugs. That argued
a prior knowledge of it. And it would represent
a sizeable piece of booty, big enough to make it a
worth-while gamble for any man. There was a better than even chance that a man like Collier, once
in possession, could go to the authorities and get
the old Spanish-Mexican titles revoked and a new
American title certified to himself.

All of which seemed to offer an ample and a
logical explanation, except for the selection of the
Ranch of the Giants itself. Jim had spent quite a
while in California, knocking about, and he had
never heard of it. So it was unlikely that Collier
would have heard of it just casually. Yet he had
known. That was a sure thing.

Behind Collier's urbane front there had been a
repressed sort of eagerness which had not been lost
on Jim. What did he really want there? Gold? If
he figured on a gold strike, he could stake claims
regardless. Plenty of men were doing that sort of
thing, regardless of property rights. Look what
was happening to Sutter, on whose land gold had

originally been found. Jim had come by there a few weeks back, visiting the newly flourishing city of Sacramento. Sutter was being crowded off his own ranch.

Mid-afternoon, on the tireless horse he rode, brought him to virtually a new world. Here were immigrants, still pouring hopefully in from the East. Here were prospectors like locusts across the land—and just as great a plague. There had been an estimated population of twenty thousand in California before the news of gold had spread. Now it was several times that number, and more were arriving every day.

Now he was coming to a sizeable camp which already called itself a town. Maybe he could find and hire some disillusioned men. He didn't want to go clear on to San Francisco if he could help it.

Gold Town! A mushroom growth, with the unlovely look and aroma of toadstools, there had been no town there a year before, nothing but unpolluted nature. Which, in Jim's opinion, was preferable to the change. But it would afford a place to stop for the night, at least. It boasted, he observed, a two-story log hotel, misnamed the Mansion House, and a few lesser accommodations. Meals were served, including fresh eggs and potatoes. The eggs, whose freshness seemed to have lost its first glow, were four bits apiece. Spuds in a sort of thick gravy made up the main course, which was an extra dollar.

Having disposed of two eggs as a side dish, Jim paid his bill and moved toward the door. He had eaten a little earlier than most of the camp, but now a jostling crowd was beginning to fill the main street as men knocked off for the day. At the door, he came abruptly face to face with Collier.

Collier was alone at the moment. At least, none of his former crew was in sight. He was as impeccably dressed as before, and only a brief flicker of surprise showed in his eyes at sight of Jim. Then, exclaiming, he held out hit hend.

"Well, well, Tobey! This is a pleasant surprise, seeing you here!"

Jim extended his own hand. It might be just as well to play the other's game for a while.

"I came out to tend to a few little things," he said easily, and became aware of a change in Collier. The sight of him had caused only a ripple of surprise which had been instantly hidden. Collier had the well trained face of a gambler. It could mask his emotions as effectively as if he had drawn a shade across it.

But something had shocked him out of his ordinary self-possession—something which now left him staring and with a sharply sucked in breath which made a small whistling noise. And his face had gone strangely white. His hand, outstretched to grasp Jim's, had faltered a few inches before their fingers touched.

With a sudden thrill, Jim saw what he was staring at so fixedly. The ring! Almost without thinking about it, he had taken it off the chain again and slipped it back on his finger. Now it was the rearing silver cayuse that held Collier's rather strained attention.

After a moment, and with a distinct effort, Collier regained control of himself, though the hot sparkle of excitement still glowed in his eyes. He shook hands, and, aware that his interest was all too apparent, made no clumsy effort to hide it.

"I hope you'll excuse my curiosity," he said, "but that ring that you're wearing gave me rather a start. It seems to be the twin to one that I owned, years ago. And lost, more's the pity."

"It is a bit unusual, isn't it?" Jim agreed.

"Decidedly." Frankness seemed to be Collier's keynote now. "Would you mind telling me where you got it? Not that I want to pry, you understand. But I didn't notice you wearing it the other day."

His disarming frankness would probably have accomplished its purpose had Jim not known more about the man than Collier suspected, including his alliance with Hank Donney and his crew. It seemed far-fetched that he could have known anything about the ring, or that it should have anything to do with his efforts to get hold of the Ranch of the Giants. On the other hand, there was something decidedly strange there. That was where Jim had first met him, and it was Jeanne who had given him the ring. His reply was casual enough.

"Oh, I just picked it up," he said. "Somebody had it, and it took my eye. You know how those things are. But I didn't wear it for a spell—guess I'm not much for jewelry, ordinary."

"Of course," Collier agreed readily—too readily. "It's unusual, isn't it?" And Jim had a swift hunch that Collier did not believe him. "Mind if I take a look at it?" he went on. "It's apparently the twin to the one I owned."

"Sure. Why not?" Jim agreed. He hid the sudden reluctance which he felt even to slip the ring off his finger. Jeanne had given it to him, and she had asked him to wear it, saying that it meant good luck. But Collier had far more than a casual interest. His excitement seemed to be increasing, not dimishing.

He turned the ring over and over in his fingers, admiring it, his eyes very quick and sharp. There was an eagerness in his voice which he could not quite cover.

"Yes sir, it's the twin to the one I used to have. That was quite a while ago—nearly a score of years. And out in this same country." He gave a quick, darting glance around, as though to reassure himself that none of the passing crowd was paying any attention, and his voice, though carefully casual still, dropped a note or so.

"I'd run away to sea, as a boy—you know how kids do those things, Tobey. Thought it would be a great adventure to sail around the world. Well, it was!" He laughed shortly. "So much so that, when I got the chance, I deserted, off the California coast, and spent a few weeks roaming around this country. It was all Spanish and Mexican then, a pretty sleepy place compared to these days. If I'd only guessed then about all the gold that was lying around loose for the finding—" He laughed again.

"I picked up a ring—a silver cayuse like this one. And then I lost it again. I've always remembered it, and regretted it. Took a real fancy to it. You wouldn't care to sell this? For a good price?"

"I'm afraid not," Jim said easily. "I kind of like it myself." He extended his hand.

Collier still twiddled it between his fingers, as if reluctant to let it go. He started to hand it back, then, with an exclamation, fumbled and dropped it. But Jim's quick motion snatched it up almost before it had hit the dust at their feet.

"Sorry," Collier said, straightening. "Clumsy of me."

"It's all right," Jim said, slipping it back on his finger. Collier, too, had made a quick, involuntary bend to snatch it again. That would be the natural thing to do, of course—though Jim had a stronger hunch than ever that the man had hoped to try a quick bit of finger-work, pretending to lose it in the dust, while really palming it. Why he should be so anxious to get hold of that old ring was puzzling. But Jim's suspicious were mounting.

For a moment Collier stared, seemingly of two

minds as to what to do, torn between desire for the ring and caution at showing it. Then he fell into step beside Jim.

"When I said that I'd buy it, I didn't expect to get it for next to nothing," he went on, with an appraising glance at Jim's down-at-heel boots and generally worn clothes. "You see, I've got a sister back East—she was just a baby when I ran away to sea. When I got back, some years later, I told her about that ring, told her that I'd gotten it in the first place because I wanted to give it to her. She always was crazy about horses. And so she's always wanted such a ring. If I could get this one for her, now— well, you see how it is. A matter of sentiment."

"Sure," Jim conceded. "But—well, it's sort of the same way with me. I feel kind of sentimental about this. Sorry to disappoint you, but I'm hangin' onto it."

"Oh, certainly, if that's the way it is." Collier appeared to drop the subject as being of no real importance. "Well, nice to have seen you, Tobey. Hope we meet again, one of these times."

He turned away, quickly losing himself in the crowd and lowering dusk. Jim clenched his fist, aware of the thick feeling of the ring. He was sud-

denly anxious to have a better look at it himself.
Since he had a room at the Mansion House, he
might as well go back.

Collier's story had sounded genuine enough. It
was hard to believe that there could be anything
unusual about this ring. But there had been, aside
from his eagerness, one false note in Collier's story.
About wanting the ring for his sister. He definitely
was not the sentimental type.

Someone lurched drunkenly against Jim, then
reached out as if to steady himself, grabbing at him.
Out of the tail of his eye, Jim Tobey saw another
man coming at him from the opposite direction.
There was no crowd at that spot; the darkness was
quite heavy.

Twisting, he evaded the other's clutching hands,
dodged also the second man who came at him. The
first man lost his appearance of drunkenness in a
flash, as he turned and jumped at him in an ominous
silence. Robbery was a common enough thing, as
Jim knew. But he was too old a hand to be caught
so easily.

He put his back to the wall of the nearest building, lashing out, not with his fists, but with his
boot. It caught the first man in the stomach as he

came at him, literally lifting him off the ground and throwing him back. He landed hard, the wind knocked out of him, and lay there, gasping, the fight gone out of him.

While the second man hesitated at this unexpected turn of events, Jim leaped at him. His fist slid along the point of the jaw, a blow which bruised his knuckles and sent his opponent staggering back. That was too much. They had been prepared for an easy victory, and this was nothing like that. The fellow turned, scuttling away in the gloom. By the time Jim swung back, the first man was getting to his feet and beating a retreat as well.

There was nothing to do about it. There was no law in most of the camps, and in any case, he could not give an accurate enough description of his assailants to do any good. In this country, you either took care of yourself, or took the consequenes. There was no middle ground.

He went on, curiously pleased with himself. He'd been in no serious trouble since recovering from the plague. For a long time, his muscles had been dead, no spring to them. Now there was. In fact, he was about as good as ever.

The big combined lobby and bar of the Mansion

House was full of a noisy crowd. California had been admitted to statehood. The news was official at last, and having just reached town, it was causing a lot of excitement. Nearly everyone there had come from some eastern state, but they had been pretty well beyond the boundaries of government lately.

Already, according to the same report, Governor Burnett and his legislature were converging on the new capital at San Jose. Some said that they were already there. It was an occasion for rejoicing.

In the excitement, Jim climbed the stairs to his own room. He struck a light and sat down to examine the ring more closely. The rearing cayuse, in heavy, bold bas-relief of pure silver—it was unusual, to say the least. And it had been turned out by some silversmith who knew his business, and was, beyond much doubt, hand-made.

But beyond that, Jim could find nothing startling about it. He replaced it on the chain, put that about his neck again, and, warmed by the thought of Jeanne and how it had lain next to her skin no longer ago than the previous night, fell asleep, untroubled by the celebration which still went on below.

He awoke, stirred by some faint sound, tensely alert. The uproar had meant nothing, but this other sound had brought him awake. As he lay in the now heavy darkness of the room, he became aware that the town had quieted, that there was now no sound from outside at all. But something like a shadow moved between him and the window.

Eight

Jim lay there, tense. He had slipped off his boots and trousers on retiring, and was attired only in his long underwear. Under it, he could still feel the roughness of the ring against his skin. And he had a sudden sharp hunch that, if someone was in that room with the purpose of robbery in mind, it must be the ring which he was after.

Would it be Collier himself, or some henchman? And was the intruder alone? It was too dark to see anything; even the shadow that had passed between him and the window was out of sight now, making no sound, no move for the moment—but perhaps getting ready to launch a sudden attack, maybe with flailing club or sticking knife. Cold sweat started on Jim's face at thought of it. He had an overly good imagination.

His fingers were exploring under his pillow, for

the Mansion House did afford a pillow to each
bed. He had put his revolver there just before
climbing into bed. But it was not there now.

Whoever had come into the room had been after
it, and had probably awakened him by slipping it
from under the pillow.

It was too dark to see anything. But on one side,
as he knew, the bed was shoved tight against the
wall. He had no choice but to get out on the other
side, and the intruder must be there, waiting, planning his next move. Jim started to toss back the
blanket, so that he would be unencumbered. Then,
with sudden inspiration, his fingers closed on opposite corners, lifting it, and he jumped up in bed,
coming to his feet.

The bed creaked, and he heard rather than saw
the reaction of the man standing there beside it,
knew that he was starting some swift movement.
Jim flung the blanket, launching himself immediately, and knew from the feel, as well as the choked
grunt, that it had enveloped the intruder, taking
him by surprise. Some instruments, perhaps the
clubed gun, raised for a chopping blow, was also
smothered by the blanket.

His leap bore the other man to the floor, with

himself uppermost. A boot raked along his leg as they thrashed wildly, and he felt the lack of his own boots. He had a momentary advantage, with the blanket and the surprise of his attack, but the intruder was a powerful man and desperate, as slippery as a freshly caught trout. He was making no sound, but he was fighting like a newly roped cayuse against the noose.

One thing was already clear to Jim. Surprised, placed at a momentary disadvantage by the blanket, this other man was not trying just to get away. He was more than willing to carry the fight to Jim, to stay right there and win it, if he could. Which argued a purpose beyond ordinary robbery.

And that purpose, Jim knew, must be the theft of the silver cayuse.

What hidden value the ring could hold for Collier, that he should be so anxious to possess it, was hard to guess. It didn't make sense. But lots of things that happened didn't. The fact was what counted.

If he had needed confirmation, it came in the way his opponent's fingers seemed to be trying to explore his own hands—feeling over them when he got the chance, as if trying to find the ring. He had pretty well rid himself of the blanket by now, and they were still locked together, there on the floor, grappling desperately. Some noise came from the hallway outside, but neither of them paid any attention to it.

The savage thrust of a knee, intended for his groin, distracted Jim's attention momentarily. He evaded it as much by instinct as anything else, found a handful of hair and jerked. That brought a grunt from his opponent, but a fist drove hard into his own face, jarring him. From beyond the door, someone was petulantly demanding to know what was going on.

Jim had no breath to waste in answer, and the other man seemed in no mood to explain. They came to their feet, and his enemy tried to stomp on his toes with booted feet. Jim danced back, repressing a howl, and lashed hard with one fist while he curled his fingers of his other hand around his opponent's neck and made sure of his target. He knew that he had hit, and hard, probably in the man's eye. And now, despite the blows which were raining back at him, he shifted his own grip, with both hands, to his enemy's throat.

Evidently several lodgers in neighboring rooms

had been disturbed by the commotion and were now gathered in the hall outside. But though he had not taken the precaution to barricade the door, which had no lock, evidently this other man had done so when first entering the room. They were shouting, shaking the door, but it held.

Jim's fingers tightened relentlessly. Staggering, locked together, they slammed into the table, and it went over with a crash. The bed shook as they bumped into it, the tramp of the other man's booted feet on the bare floorboards was loud. The noise outside was increasing, as the others tried to force the door.

And now, Jim knew with grim satisfaction, his opponent was getting more than he had bargained for. He was alternately flailing at Jim's head and chest with his fists, or trying to tear those clutching fingers away from his throat. There was frenzy in him, his breath had been almost all shut away. He found Jim's hair and jerked, his boots kicked and raked, but, head lowered, hands like talons, Jim increased his pressure. This was, it wouldn't be long.

His enemy knew it. He made a last frantic effort to break away, jerking back, and his body hit the window and was through it with a crashing of glass. Then he was falling, tearing loose despite all that Jim could do. Jim heard a thud as he struck, down below, another crash as the door finally burst open to a concerted attack and men surged in with lanterns.

Straightening, Jim saw that the room was a shambles. And for the moment he was in little better shape. He could judge that from the way in which the others fell abruptly silent, staring at him. There was blood on his face, he guessed, and he had taken a lot of punishment in the last few minutes. But he could still feel the uneven roughness of the silver cayuse against his skin.

Something reflected the lights from the floor. The Colt which he had taken from Hank Donney, which had been under his pillow. Evidently the would-be robber had lost it in the surprise of Jim's first attack with the blanket. That had probably had a heavy bearing on the outcome of the fight.

The others were exclaiming now, questioning. They saw the smashed window and went to lean out. But whoever had taken that tumble to the ground below had still been able to get to his feet and run, and the night had swallowed him. Belatedly, someone thought to clatter down the stairs and around outside, but Jim knew that it was wasted effort.

He saw no familiar face in the crowd. These men were friendly, roused by the noise of the battle, questioning him sympathetically now. Only the landlord, who had now appeared, looked morosely at the broken door, the smashed window and the broken furniture, and did not seem too well pleased.

Robberies were common enough, but they did not often take place in a hotel room. Excitement cooled, the others departed. After dressing, Jim sat down on the edge of the bed to think it over.

He was convinced now that the ring had been the object of the attempted robbery. No other explanation seemed to fit. If he had been a miner, with a newly made strike, or known to have won a lot of money by gambling, it would have been different. But none of those explanations fitted his case. Here, no one but Collier knew him. And there was no reason for any would-be robber to go out of his way to pick on him. That would be taking too long a chance, with too slight a prospect of getting anything of value.

Yet what value could there be to the ring, to justify such an attempt? Aside from its oddness, it would be worth only a few dollars at most. It was a puzzle.

He had planned to shave this morning, and the gray light of day was already stealing in at the window. So, stubbornly enough, though his face was bruised and sore, he started to shave. It took enough extra time so that breakfast was being served by the time he was ready for it.

The camp was quiet enough at that hour. But the exciting news that California was now a state was still running through it like a thread of gold in quartz. It seemed, overnight, to have brought a change with it.

Gold fever was still running high, and would continue to do so, at least as long as new strikes were being made, and the irresistible wash of new prospectors continued to roll in from the East, or arrive by ship from the Coast. But gold had been the main desire of most of the newcomers up to now, the one fevered thought in their heads.

Now a new and more sober mood was possessing some of them, prompted partly by the disillusionment which comes with failure, partly by the news.

They had all been long enough absent from their old homes to lose their citizenship and voting rights in those states. But most of them could claim new citizenship and voting rights here, and if California was a state, that would mean something.

Citizenship in a state was something substantial. This was no longer just a mining camp. There were other things than gold, and there would be other ways to make a living. Something of that, though not voiced, seemed to be in the soberer thinking of many a man that day.

Jim found a knot of men talking on a corner. The men who had claims thereabouts had already gone to them, and most of the idlers, after a boisterous night, were still asleep. These men belonged to neither class. Jim knew them. They had been hard-working men back home—farmers, blacksmiths, storekeepers. Here they were on their uppers, out of work, yet old habit made them rise with the sun.

"Any of you boys want a job?" he asked.

They looked at him, noting that he had been in a fight, sizing him up. Quietly, in the way that most men learned to do with strangers, after getting that far across the turbulent road. Then the face of one of them, a big man with a wild thatch of hair, brightened.

"B'golly, if'n it ain't Jim Tobey!" he exclaimed. "Don't you 'member me, Jim?"

"Sure I do," Jim agreed, his own recognition clicking at the same moment. "You were doin' some blacksmithin', back at the Blue. Worked on my wagon. Let's see. Said you were broke, and tryin' to make enough to keep going, so's you could get your share of the gold. I got it. Bob Reese. You got that gold yet?"

Reese grinned.

"Been out here goin' on a year now, and I'm broker'n I was back at the Blue," he confessed. "I've worked and made me two grub-stakes, and used them up—and ain't found enough gold to put in your eye. Like these boys here. Sure there's gold in Californy—but way it looks to me, there's a dozen men lookin' for every nugget that's in the ground."

"Yeah," one of the others agreed. "And I'm through bein' a durned fool and huntin' for it. Did you say somethin' about a job?"

Here was what he had been looking for. Half a dozen men who had had their fill of prospecting and wanted jobs. With Bob Reese to head them—and he knew Reese for an honest man. Jim hired them promptly, explaining what he wanted, and they accepted without demur.

"Don't know's I c'n lay claim to bein' no cowhand," Reese said. "But I can learn, I guess. This last year or so I learnt to do more things than I ever dreamt I could, than I even knew they was things to do."

That was the way with most of them. On the road west they had learned to ride and handle stock, even those who had been strangers to all that before. Four of the six had horses of their own. Jim got hold of cayuses for the others, and gave his instructions.

"You should reach the ranch by night," he said. "Here's a letter from me, telling about you. And here's what I want you to do."

He explained about the Ranch of the Giants, and *Señor* Gonzales, and how his crew had deserted him. He touched lightly on his meeting with Jeanne, but detailed the arrival of Hank Donney and his cutthroat crew, the subsequent appearance on the scene of Collier, and how he had discovered him to be in league with Donney.

"No tellin' when they'll be trying some fresh deviltry," he added. "So be on the watch. And there's a lot of hay, ripe now, but better'n nothing. You get it cut and put up, 'fore snow flies. That's the first important job. Get at it. I'll be back pretty soon—maybe today, maybe not for a few days. Depends on how things work out. Till I get there, you go ahead and run the job, Bob. I'm countin' on you boys."

"We won't waste no time," Reese promised, and, with a lighter heart, Jim saw them out. By rights, he knew, he should go along with them. He had come out to get a crew, and he'd been lucky. Here it was.

So there was really nothing to keep him from going back with them, and plenty of work to do when he got there. Besides, he was anxious—he admitted it, rather gravely, to himself—to get back there and see Jeanne again, to make sure that everything was all right.

The thought of her was warming. Never before had he had anybody to come home to. Still, he wasn't much worried about the situation, because Collier was there in town, and he didn't believe that Collier would try anything which might cause direct trouble against the ranch—not right away, at least. The man had some other, more oblique scheme in mind.

On the other hand, the knowledge that Jim was away from it might make him change his plans. But if so, Reese and the others should arrive there as soon as any of Collier's gang.

He could start back now—probably he would, before the day was much older. But what he really wanted to do was to look around and see if he could find Collier first. To see whether Collier showed the marks of having been in a fight during the night. And if he did—well, he might have another battle on his hands. Jim felt in just the mood right now to choke the truth out of him—the truth about the silver cayuse.

Nine

Wearing the ring boldly on his finger now, Jim hung around town for a little while, making a few discreet inquiries which told him nothing. Then, impatient, he decided to return to the ranch. If Collier was still interested, he would show up there again, sooner or later.

He was just nicely out of town, around a brush-bordered bend of the road, when he saw her.

She was lying there, sprawled in the dusty grass beside the road, a crumpled little heap which stirred and groaned and tried to raise herself on one hand as he came in sight, then fell back again. Her hat, a sort of bonnet affair, lay several feet away, and her hair had become loosened, so that it shone in full glory. And shone was the word. It was the darkest, yet somehow most vivid red that Jim had ever seen.

His horse shied and snorted, but Jim swung it back and dismounted. The girl, he figured, must have been riding there alone. Evidently her horse had thrown her, and she was hurt.

She tried to rise again, as he bent above her, and succeeded this time in partly lifting herself on one hand, turning her face up to him. Wide blue eyes looked into his own; a smudge of dirt ran across her nose and one cheek. He put his hands under her arms and helped her to sit up.

"Take it easy," he adjured. "You'll be all right."

Panting a little, she bit her lip, holding it for a moment between strong white teeth as if to steady her nerves. She reached out unsteady fingers to straighten her dress a little, so that it would reveal less of a shapely ankle underneath. Her eyes were still wide.

"W-what happened?" she asked.

"Looks to me like your horse must have tossed you off," Jim said reasonably.

She nodded, still looking up at him.

"My horse? Yes, that was it. I remember now—something scared it, and he jumped sidewise—and I guess I went off. I'm not much of a rider, any-way." Unsteadily, she started to get to her feet, and then sank back with a little moan. "My foot! It hurts!"

Jim examined it as well as he could without removing the shoe.

"It seems to be all right," he said doubtfully. "I don't believe it's broken."

"Probably not," she agreed. "But it hurts. I can't walk. And I was to meet Aunt Lyddy at her place for breakfast—she'll be worried sick about me."

"Where does your Aunt Lyddy live?" Jim asked practically. He was trying to keep his mind on the business at hand, and off such distracting things as red hair and a well turned ankle.

"Oh—" She looked around, studying their surroundings. "About a mile and a half from here, I guess it is. Off down that side road. She and Uncle Oscar have a claim, and a little house. Uncle Oscar's away for a couple of days, and I was to go out and stay with her—"

"If you feel all right, you can ride my horse," Jim suggested. "I'll be glad to take you there."

"Oh, would you?" The smile, which she gave him made his breath come a little faster. "It's awfully kind of you. I guess I could ride—a gentle horse. With you to help me. And you don't even know my name. I'm Alice Osburn."

"I'm Jim Tobey," he said. "Here, I'll help you to the saddle."

He did so, half lifting her, while her disarranged hair came completely loose and fell over both of them. It was long hair, with a faint, curiously pleasant fragrance, he noted, and felt that his own face must be nearly as red as her hair. Her own cheeks were scarlet as she gathered at it quickly, nervously.

"Oh, I'm all coming to pieces, and every which-way," she gasped. "If you'll just be so kind as to hand me up my bonnet there, I'll try and tuck it in."

Presently a little order was restored, and they turned up the side road, Jim leading the horse. It was, he noticed, a little used trail, with considerable brush and trees on either side. They had gone a quarter of a mile when a creek, hidden by the brush, scurried past, its silver gleam barely visible through the foliage. Somewhere close, but out of sight, it took a considerable fall, and the noise of the waterfall was so loud at that spot that it was necessary almost to shout if they wanted to talk.

He was looking up at her, trying to make himself heard, when men burst out of the brush on either side of the road and came at him—at least three of them. Too late, Jim realized that he had been led into a trap. Such a thing as this did not happen by accident. If any doubt had remained in his mind, it was swept away as she instantly leaned forward and, snatching the reins into her own hands, expertly swung the horse aside, out of the way—so that one of the attackers could get at him more easily.

Two of them he had never seen before, but the third had been with Hank Donney in the attack on the ranch. This was another scheme on the part of Collier to get that silver cayuse ring, and he had walked readily enough into the trap. True, it had been clever enough, and well baited.

These thoughts flashed through his mind in the first second or so. Then he was tense, alert, and ready. The very haste of the first two to get at him gave him an advantage. He stuck out a foot and tripped the first man, and as the second man tried to keep from stumbling over the fallen man in turn, Jim had a good opening, and he made the most of it. His fist caught this second man just behind the ear, and he went down, sprawling across the first man, who was trying to scramble up again.

Jim swung about, his hand going to his holstered gun. If these fellows wanted trouble, he was just in the mood to give it to them. He had the gun in his hand when something seemed to explode in his skull, and his knees went shaky.

Dimly he sensed that there had been a fourth man, whom he had not seen before—someone wary enough to linger in the brush, not showing himself until the critical moment. Then he had stepped out and smashed Jim across the skull with a club, or something like it.

Quite plainly they expected him to go down then. He was groggy, out on his feet. But there was fury in him, and a determination not to quit. Somehow he stayed up, and kept on fighting. He turned, caught the club in his own hands as the other man tried to strike again, and wrested it away with a sort of insane strength. He had no conscious knowledge of what he was doing. The wild fury of his onslaught temporarily drove the others back, appalled, and his head cleared a little, a bit of the weakness in his legs disappeared.

Then they were at him again, all four of them

now, a wild pack driven by a desperate fury to match his own. He was beaten to his knees, and dimly he heard the voice of the man who had been with Hank Donney, urging the others on. Urging them to kill him.

They would, in another few minutes, at that rate. He was just about finished, past the power to fight any longer. Blood was in his eyes, blinding him; the world swam monstrously and seemed to spin and twist. And then, when he expected a shot or a finishing blow, they all fell back, leaving him or a blow, they all fell back, leaving him alone. completely at a loss to account for it. Was it some sort of a trick? And then, as from a long way off, he heard the voice of the red-haired girl—a little high and shrill, as if half hysterical, yet with a deadly, biting quality to it as well.

"Leave him alone, I tell you! Beasts! Murderers! I thought you only wanted to rob him—not to kill him. Get away before I shoot!"

It didn't make sense, of course—none of it did. But it was happening. That was the way with life. You expected one thing, and prepared for it, and something else happened.

He raised his head, and saw that the red-head,

sitting in the saddle with practiced ease and controlling his skittish horse with a quite unconscious hand on the reins, was holding a revolver in her other hand, and menacing the four with it. And looking at her, at the fury which flamed in her eyes to match her hair, he found it easy to believe that she would shoot without hesitation.

Plainly the others believed it, too. One of them started to mutter a protest, then fell silent as she swung the gun more directly at him.

"Git!" she snapped. "Before I fill all of you full of lead!"

They hesitated briefly. Then one of them turned and took to his heels, and that example was enough for the others. Seeing that Jim was recovering, getting back up from his knees again, and with the unpredictable red-head waving a gun at them, they plunged into the brush and out of sight.

Jim's head was still ringing, aching, and he felt sick and sore all over. But the ring, he realized vaguely, was still on his finger. He had felt somebody trying to jerk it off, but had clenched his fist and fought the harder. Dazedly, irrationally, he remembered what Jeanne had told him—that wearing the ring would bring him good luck!

Well, if the things that had been happening lately were a sample of it, he wasn't so sure. It certainly wasn't the sort of luck that he'd go out of his way to find. But there must be something about the silver cayuse, strange as it seemed, that Collier also regarded as being lucky, considering the lengths to which he was going to try and get hold of it.

The red-head was staring down at him now, a strange play of emotions across her face. Astonishment, as if she were just now realizing what she had done and could not quite understand herself. Anger, which still seethed against the quartette, pity, and a kind of bleak disgust for herself. Something of all that was in her voice when she spoke.

"You'll hate me, of course—I don't blame you. But they were only to rob you—I never hired out to lead you to your death! And they were going to kill you!"

She closed her eyes tightly for a moment, and her face went white. Jim thought that she was going to faint. But it was not that. She opened her eyes again, and the emotion of self-disgust, of repugnance at what she was and what she had done was strongest of all now.

"Here," she whispered, and slipped out of the saddle with the same easy expertness that he had noted before. She thrust the reins into his hands, turned, and in her turn plunged away into the sheltering brush. Something like a choked sob came back to him.

The voice of the waterfall was as loud as before, and it was easy to tell why that spot had been chosen. The side trail, where no one ever came, the waterfall to drown any noise, and a body could be slung into the deep pool at the foot of the fall and forgotten. That was the way it had been planned, with the girl hired to act as bait for the trap.

Reaction was setting in now. His own fury and desperate desire to keep fighting against the inevitable fate that had seemed about to overtake him had kept him going before. Now that it was all over, the punishment that he had taken was having its effect. He was sick, dizzy, so weak that he could hardly stand. He reached out and got hold of the saddle and clung fast for a minute, barely able to hang on. Then, knowing that if he waited he'd never make it, he dragged himself into the saddle and gave his horse its head. It wouldn't do to wait there—not in that shape. Some of Collier's wolf-pack might come sneaking back.

The ride was like a dream. He opened his eyes, aware of the hot sun on his head, conscious that his horse had stopped. Then he saw that it had returned to the livery stable where it had spent the night. He got down, managing to walk stiffly, and went in. There was nobody around for the moment, but there were plenty of empty stalls. He left his horse in one, removing the bridle, pulling off the saddle in a mechanical sort of way. There was a haymow off a little way, and he crossed to it, to the far side where no one could see him, and stretched out.

The buzzing of flies about his face awoke him. There was a little window high up, and the sun came through it and reached down and seemed to concentrate its rays upon him, and so the flies had been attracted by the dried blood upon him. It must be late afternoon, he decided, as his head cleared a little. He had slept for several hours.

Hunger made itself felt now. He was stiff and sore, but otherwise he felt considerably better. He'd been in a bad way, but not too bad, when the redhead had suffered a change of heart. He thought about her, in a curiously detached way. She had betrayed him, doing it deliberately and for hire. But she had saved his life, because she hadn't expected him to be hurt any worse than might be necessary for purposes of robbery. To that odd contradiction he owed his life, and the one act pretty well wiped out the other.

In any case, he'd probably never see her again, so that was nothing to worry about. He stood up, and saw that his horse was still there. The big barn still seemed empty, but there was a watering-trough, with a pump at one end.

He went to it, pumped the trough full, then sank his face in the coolness, drinking deep, washing as well as he could. That made him feel vastly better. He'd spend the night there in town, he decided, and see what Collier might try next, if anything. It was a little funny that nobody had noticed him come in, nor bothered him during the day. Certainly, for a while, he'd been in no shape to do anything about it.

Right now, he'd go and get some supper. He stepped outside, blinking a little in the sunshine, and stopped suddenly. Apparently it was as much of a surprise to her as to himself, but again he had come face to face with the red-head.

Ten

Her hand went to her mouth in a quick instinctive gesture, and her face whitened, her eyes widened. Again, as in the morning, he noted how very blue they were, by contrast with her hair.

For a moment they stood, neither one quite sure of what to say or do. It was she who spoke, with what seemed a sudden resolution.

"You hate me, of course," she said. "And I don't blame you. But—but I'd like to talk to you, for just a minute—to tell you something—something that you'd ought to know—" She hesitated again, then added, "About Collier."

The town was becoming crowded. Not so much so as it would be an hour from then, when most of the miners knocked off work for the day and started in to relax. But right there the street was quiet enough, for the moment. Jim nodded.

"You saved my neck for me, at the end," he said. "Guess that makes up for the other."

There was a sudden eagerness in her face now, like that of a condemned man just hearing news of a reprieve.

"I hate myself," she said fiercely. "I'm no good! But it was just to be robbery—and he said that the ring really belonged to him—"

"I thought that was what it was about," Jim nodded.

"Yes, it was the ring he wanted," she agreed. "But I—I'm not that low—not yet—to lead a man to his death. Especially after the way you'd just tried to help me. But there's more than the ring. I heard him talking, this morning—there's a ranch mixed up in it somewhere, isn't there? A big Spanish ranch?"

"There seems to be," Jim agreed.

"Well—I don't know just what it's all about. But California's a state now, you know. And Spanish titles aren't too good, these days. I heard him say that he was going to San Jose to see the Governor, and the legislature, to get them to give him the title to this ranch. He said something else about you, so that I knew that you were connected with the ranch, too. Then he took the stage for San Jose, this afternoon."

She looked at him for a moment, and there was a desperate earnestness in her face.

"I don't know whether it's important or not—" Her voice sank almost to a whisper. "Maybe you think this is another trap. But I wanted to tell you. I—I had to do that much."

She turned abruptly, was away and down the street and around a corner almost before he knew what she was about. Jim stared after her for a moment, his mind busy with what she had just told him. He knew that she would not come back. It would be sheer chance if they ever met again. But she had been anxious to make amends, insofar as she could, for what had happened that morning.

He had seen other women like her, there in the frontier country. They far outnumbered other women. But Alice Osburn at least, was a long way from being all bad. Given a new start and half a chance, she had it in her to amount to something.

The fact that Collier had gone on to San Jose accounted for the fact that things had been calm in town that day. A man as suave and cultured as Collier appeared to be could easily find a way to influence the governor and the legislature to do what he wanted. He'd know the right sort of a story to tell them. He had boasted, too, that he knew the governor.

And, as the red-head had said, old Spanish titles, especially those issued to old Spanish or Mexican grandees, were not too good in those hectic days when the young state was feeling its oats.

Something had made Collier decide that getting unquestioned possession of the Ranch of the Giants was of paramount importance. If it was vital to him, Jim decided, then it was equally vital to checkmate him.

He went into a restaurant and ate, noting that no one paid much attention to him. With a good meal under his belt, he felt better, and considered whether to take his own horse and ride for San Jose or not. But he decided against it. He was still tired and far from being in good shape, and if he rode all night, he'd be in no condition to see anyone the next day. Besides, business such as that would take more than one day to consummate.

With Collier gone, there seemed little likelihood of anyone bothering him that night, but he decided to sleep in the hay again, slipping back into the stable when no one was around to see him. When he came out in the morning, the stableman eyed him in sleepy surprise.

"I'm leavin' my horse here a few days," Jim explained, and went on to breakfast.

Again, as on the previous day, the town was nearly deserted at that hour. But a few were gathered when the stage appeared presently—a rather descrepit-looking affair, far short of the Concords which were now in service between Sacramento, San Francisco and the capital. But it was a big improvement over the freight wagons which until very recently had carried passengers from Sonora to San Jose, offering the only available accommodations.

It was late afternoon when they came to San Jose. This was all new to Jim, and he viewed it with the lively interest of a fiddle-footed man. He had seen Sacramento and San Francisco, without being too much impressed by either of them. San Francisco was a sprawling, overgrown and overcrowded shack town, and Sacramento's chief interest, in his eyes, lay in the fact that it was there that Sutter had held semifeudal sway, a rich man, until gold had been found on his land. And gold, while it had enriched others and thrown the world into turmoil, was ruining Sutter.

San Jose was, like many another town, being transformed from a sleepy little village to a rushing, mushrooming metropolis. A two-story, adobe state house was under process of construction. The town was even more overcrowded than the camp from which he had just come.

The stage disgorged its passengers at Pat Welch's livery stable, and Jim turned toward the City Hotel just opposite it. He got a supper which made him wish for his own cooking, or that of Margarita with Jeanne serving him, and when he asked for a room was told that he was lucky. Ordinarily there were no rooms.

"But we c'n accommodate you, stranger," the clerk assured him. "Just due to a piece of luck. Sign the book here, will you? There was a shootin' in town, not a quarter of an hour ago. Mebby you heard it?"

"I heard a couple of shots," Jim acknowledged.

"Yeah. That was it. Wa'al, the feller that had yore room, he won't be needin' it any more. I just saw them packin' him off to the undertaker's. Packed a big gun, but like a lot of these tenderfeet, he didn't know rightly how to use it. Mighty poor insurance, that way." His manner became brisk. "He won't be wantin' the room any more, so you're lucky."

The governor was in town, all right. Everybody attested to that. So, too, were most of his legislature—already becoming known as the Legislature of a Thousand Drinks. With such a bunch of lawmakers, Jim reflected, Collier should be in his element.

In his room, he shaved, making himself as presentable as possible. Usually, from what he had been able to learn, Governor Burnett was rather reserved, though friendly, and accustomed to keeping pretty much to himself. But being new in town, Jim learned that he was circulating around that evening, greeting old acquaintances and making new ones. Since the main gathering places were saloons, he might be lucky enough to run across him in one of them.

If he could, it might be a better time to approach him than during the business day. He could buy a few drinks himself, if that approach should be helpful, though with the governor it probably would not be.

The streets, as well as the buildings, were thronged now. It was that way in every town and camp where miners could come. There was gold in California—and though only a handful were finding it, its golden fever made hot the blood of the entire community. Everybody who had money was spending it as though anxious to be rid of it again, gambling, drinking, dispensing with a lavish hand.

On the street, Jim halted, his eyes narrowing. Yes, there was no mistake. That was Collier off there—and though he was as carefully groomed as ever, one eye still looked as if it might have had quite a shiner, say the day before. Beefsteak had gotten it almost back to normal, but not quite.

That was no surprise, but it was nice to have his hunch confirmed that it had been Collier who had tried to rob him in his room. He started to push his way across to Collier, but the crowd was too thick, and Collier soon disappeared. Jim doubted if he had seen him and slipped away. He had the feeling that Collier would have had just enough cold nerve to wait for him, if he had seen him.

He was carrying the silver cayuse ring on the chain again now, out of sight. Of late, he had taken to noticing the hands of other men to see if they wore rings or not, and if they did, he had observed the rings. For his part, he had never been one for any sort of jewelry or personal adornment up to then, and he was a little surprised at the number of men who did wear rings. Gamblers flashed diamonds, and there was an occasional odd or striking design. But nothing that resembled the silver cayuse.

His curiosity about it was mounting. What sort of a value could it have, that Collier should go to such extreme lengths to try to get hold of it? Collier had ascribed his desire to sentiment, but Jim placed no credence in that story. Collier wasn't that sort of a man.

But Collier was the only man who seemed really to know anything about it. That was one more reason—out of a mounting list—he had to have a showdown with Collier, and get a few answers from him, one of these days.

Right now, however, he wanted to find the governor. He drifted to a big new saloon, and asked a casual question or so. The answer was revealing.

"Yes, quite a distinguished crowd here tonight. At least a dozen members of the legislature—" His informant pointed out several who were visible. "And there's Governor Burnett himself over there."

Jim studied him, A tall, spare man, he looked rugged enough. He had an oblong face, dark hair, and was engaged at the moment in telling some story to a circle gathered about him.

As soon as he could, and once the circle had broken up, Jim made his way across to where the governor now sat at a little table. He was again greeting friends and acquaintances, relaxing and enjoying himself. People kept coming and going. Then the governor arose and was presently standing near the bar, talking. Taking advantage of his opportunity, Jim placed himself at Burnett's elbow.

"There's a lot of money bein' spent here, for a brand-new capital in a brand-new state," he ventured.

"You've said it, my friend," the governor agreed heartily. "But California is no ordinary state. I don't believe I've had the pleasure of meeting you before, have I?"

"Nope, I guess not," Jim agreed. "I'm Jim Tobey." Watching narrowly, he saw no change in Burnett's expression. If Collier had talked with him during the day, he apparently had not mentioned Jim. "I'm foreman for a big ranch back in the mountains," he went on casually, "in to see the sights. Ranch of the Giants," he added off-handedly.

This time, he did see the sudden flicker in the governor's eyes. It was plain that he had heard of the Ranch of the Giants.

"In fact, your excellency," Jim went on, "I'd sure appreciate a chance to talk about that ranch with you, at yore convenience. It's owned by a fine old Spanish fam'ly, who have their titles direct in line from the days when the King of Spain gave away titles to big estates. But the way things are these days, unsettled and all—and with some of our more unscrupulous feller-countrymen showin' a disregard for any sort of law—I'd like to make sure that there won't be no trouble about their title."

The governor heard him through, though with uplifted hand and purpling face. It was only too apparent to Jim that Collier had already talked with Burnett, and that he had, as was to be expected, made a favorable impression.

"Unscrupulous fellow-countrymen!" Burnett

spluttered. "Sir, I've no time for such a matter—positively no time at all! I have heard something of this Ranch of the Giants, as it happens, and I am convinced that this ancient title is like a lot of these old Mexican titles—in fact, no title at all."

"I take it that you've been listening to Collier today?" Jim said bluntly.

"A gentleman of the name of Collier has talked with me, yes—"

"A skunk would be a more fittin' word for him, Governor. Though I'll admit he has a fancy way of talkin'—"

"Not another word!" The governor was furious. "This is monstrous, Mr. Tobey. To come to me and slander a gentleman of his repute behind his back. The matter is already settled, and not subject to reopening. I—"

"Do you mean to tell me," Jim cut in hotly, "that you hear just one side of a story and make your decision, and won't even listen to the other side? Is that your notion of the way to run a state?"

It was not, he knew, the proper tone to take to the governor. But his temper was getting out of bounds. Unconsciously, almost, he had slipped the ring off the chain and onto his finger again while he talked. Now he wagged his finger in the governor's apoplectic face.

"I came here, intendin' to try and see that some poor old folks, who've been decent citizens all their days, and whose only crime seems to be that California has changed ownership, got a fair deal," he went on. "And do you mean to tell me, as governor, that both sides to a case can't get that?"

He doubted if his words were going to have any effect, other than to inflame the governor further. But something was producing the desired effect. And then he saw, with mounting incredulity, that the governor was staring at the silver cayuse on his finger, his eyes fairly popping as he viewed it. His voice was changed, a little hoarse.

"Where did you get that ring?" he demanded. "We—let's go where we can talk this all over, Mr. Tobey, without interruption."

Eleven

The governor led the way, his tall, spare figure very upright, with only an abstracted nod or wave of the hand to acquaintances who greeted him. Jim was thinking fast. What was there about this ring, that it could first affect Collier so, then have such an upsetting effect upon the governor? It didn't seem to fit—but there it was. And here, perhaps, was some of the good luck which was supposed to go with the ring. Certainly Burnett had been about to conclude the interview, to refuse to discuss the ranch further. Now he was very much interested.

Governor Burnett said nothing as they went down the street and across to a private room in the hotel. Only after the door had been closed behind them and he had motioned Jim to a seat did he speak again. He had regained control of himself now, but it was evident that he was still laboring under considerable excitement.

"Would you mind letting me have another look at that ring, please?"

"Of course," Jim agreed. He drew it off his finger, tendered it. The governor examined it carefully, then handed it back.

"No doubt of it," he said. "It's the Silver Cayuse. Would you mind telling me where—or when—you got hold of this ring, Mr. Tobey?"

"I've no objections," Jim agreed. "As I was startin' to tell you in regard to the Ranch of the Giants, for several generations it has been in the possession of the Gonzales. They have an adopted daughter, Jeanne. Near as I could find out, they don't know what her last name was, nor just who her parents were, except that they were Americans. But seems that when she was pretty small, her dad and ma was killed by Indians. Or anyway, that's what they figure, for somebody done them in. The Gonzales found the little girl, and took and raised her like she'd been their own."

Governor Burnett was following him closely now. He nodded.

"Please go on," he said.

116

"Well, I was able to help the Gonzales and Jeanne a few days ago—I'd like to tell you more about that, pretty soon. Anyway, they gave me the job of foreman of the ranch. Most of their crew had deserted to dig for gold, and we had to have a crew, so I started out ti try and rustle one up. When I got ready to leave, Jeanne handed me this ring, and said that it had belonged to her pa. Told me it was supposed to be good luck, and asked me to wear it."

The governor had been listening attentively, but his face was expresisonless now. How much of the story he was accepting at face value, it was hard to tell. Jim was resolved to find out.

"I've met one other man who seemed to recognize the ring—and to take a lot of interest in it," he added bluntly. "He calls himself Gregory Collier."

"Eh?" The ejaculation seemed to be torn from the governor despite himself.

"Exactly," Jim said a little dryly. "And now, with your permission, I'd like to tell you the rest of my story, as it concerns this ring and the ranch."

This time the governor did not hesitate.

"I shall be glad to hear it," he agreed.

Jim lost no time. He explained how he had come

to the vicinity of the big ranch, how Jeanne had gotten acquainted with him, and about her appeal for help, which he had answered. Of Collier's arrival, after Hank Donney and his men had been made prisoners, and of how Collier had offered to take the prisoners off their hands and turn them over to the law. Also, of how he had offered to buy the ranch.

Governor Burnett heard him in silence. Now he frowned.

"But I see nothing irregular in the conduct of Mr. Collier, as you relate it," he protested.

"Neither did I—up to then," Jim drawled. "But I smelt a skunk. When he started off down the road with Donney and his crew, I made out to head off up in the hills, in the other direction. Took good care that he'd see me. Then I swung, keepin' just out of sight, and circled. Got to the road, a couple of miles off, just before they come along. And just about that time, it turned out he was in cahoots with Donney, same as I'd had a hunch."

"How do you mean?"

"They'd all been whistlin' one certain tune, off and on, up at the ranch—Collier's men had. Sounded to me like it might be a signal—and who'd it be for, if not Donney and his bunch? Well, like I say, I saw them comin' along. Then they stopped. Collier said it wasn't needful for Donney to stay tied up no longer. Made fun of him for tryin' to grab a ranch from a handful of unsuspectin' old folks, and not makin' good at it. It was easy to tell that Donney had been hired by Collier to come and get hold of the ranch for him. Only he'd bungled the job."

"Those are serious charges, Mr. Tobey."

"Yeah. Only they happen to be the truth. You wanted to know about things, and I'm tellin' you. Ain't it about on a par with Collier's comin' to you and wantin' you to invalidate the Gonzales' old title and give the ranch to him?"

The governor pursed his lips and frowned.

"You still have something to tell?" he suggested.

"Quite a bit. Collier turned 'em loose—said he'd get hold of the ranch another way he had in mind, and they all went on together. Knowin' what they was up to—though I hadn't thought about Collier comin' to you—I figgered the best thing was to go out and hire a crew to do the work on the ranch, and to defend it with. I started, and Jeanne, she gave me the ring. I got to Gold Town, and found Collier there. He didn't know that I was on to him, and we talked, friendly enough. He was plumb int'rested in this ring. Wanted to buy it. Gave a right funny story as his reason."

"Yes?" Governor Burnett's interest seemed to quicken again. So Jim repeated the story, as closely as he could.

"I wasn't int'rested," he added. "So he made two-three tries then to get hold of it—by robbery, or murder." He went on again to recount what had happened, and he saw the deepening incredulity in the governor's eyes. Some of this, he knew, did sound rather incredible. Only it happened to be the truth, and he was going to stick to the truth, no matter how wild it might appear.

"That's my story," he added bluntly. "I've told things as they happened. And if you took a look at Collier, you could see that he'd been in a fight right recent. And now I'd like to know why a look at this ring got you all excited. What's there about it that has such an effect on you—not to mention a gent like Collier?"

This time, the governor seemed more friendly.

"That's a reasonable question," he agreed. "And I'll tell you what I know. Which isn't much. Have you ever heard anything about that ring—or others like it—aside from what you've told me?"

"Nary a thing."

"Not many people in California have, I suppose," the governor conceded. "Nearly everybody out here now is a newcomer in the last year or so, of course—since the discovery of gold. But if you'd been here fifteen or twenty years ago, as Collier claims to have been, it would have been a different story."

"I was a little young for bein' here, then," Jim drawled.

Peter Burnett smiled.

"I wouldn't doubt it. For my part, I don't know any of this from personal experience, you understand. It's only what I've been told, but from authentic sources. Not many weeks ago, I happened to see a twin to the ring which you are wearing, which was a keepsake. It was so odd that it intrigued me, and I asked questions. And the story connected with those rings—there were originally perhaps a dozen, or maybe a score of them—was as odd as what you've been telling me."

"I'd sure like to hear it," Jim said.

"I'll tell you what I know. Twenty years or so

121

ago, back in the early thirties, California was of course under Mexican rule. A very sleepy, peaceful place on the whole, I guess, with few Americans or other foreigners, and no thought of gold. But an occasional ship touched here, and sailors—men like Collier described himself to you as being then—came ashore. Some of them deserted. Anyway, there was a lawless element, made up partly, I gather, of the native element as well. They robbed and murdered and instituted quite a reign of terror for a while, according to report."

"Reckon Collier would fit right in with that."

"He might, if what you've told me is accurate," the governor conceded cautiously. "At all events, there was such a gang, terrorizing a large section of the country. So, as I have the story, certain determined men, owners of ranches and others of position, determined to stamp out the reign of lawlessness. They banded together secretly—in a sort of vigilance society, I would say. And to make sure of positive identification, since they were widely scattered and many did not know the others, they hit upon the idea of wearing a ring, of a special design."

"The Silver Cayuse!" Jim breathed.

"Exactly. Some silversmith of considerable skill made the rings. There were a dozen or perhaps twenty members, but not more than that. I don't know much more about it, I'm sorry to say. It seems, however, that they were quite effective in stamping out the lawless element. Quite a few bandits were shot or otherwise disposed of, the gang broken up. Naturally, after seeing another such a ring recently, and hearing the story, I was more than a little amazed to see you wearing one like it."

"And that's all you know about the ring?"

"That's all I know. But it was enough to get a hearing for you."

"I'm glad of that, and it's a mighty int'restin' story." Jim nodded. "But it strikes me that Collier likely knows a lot more than that about these rings. If he was connected with the gang, back in those days, he'd have had a chance to learn plenty, likely."

"That seems logical enough. Though it's quite possible that he was one of the vigilance committee."

Jim shook his head.

"Not that hombre, Governor. He looks like

turkey—but he's just plain turkey buzzard. He gave me a nice-soundin' story, but sentiment don't int'rest him none. There's somethin' else—some secret connected with this silver cayuse that he's mighty int'rested in. Enough so that he was willing to murder to get hold of it."

For a moment, the governor drummed thoughtfully on the arm of his chair.

"Perhaps you are right," he conceded. "It's entirely possible that such a ring did hold some sort of a secret to the few initiates in the order. I've never heard of such a thing, but it might be. You are making serious charges against Collier, of course."

"When a man tries to kill me, I figure I know his stripe pretty well," Jim said dryly. He leaned abruptly forward.

"You told me, first off, that this matter of the ranch was all settled already. You didn't mean that, did you? I'd hate to think that California law, now it's a part of the United States, did things in such a fashion as that—or that you did either, Governor."

Burnett looked a little unhappy.

"Frankly, I was angry at you—at what seemed to me a wholly unwarranted intrusion and assumption on your part," he conceded. "But I was over-simplifying a bit. It isn't settled yet."

"I guess I was kind of assumin'," Jim nodded. "But I had to talk to you—and after all that'd been happening', it kind of made me mad."

"I can appreciate that. Let me make myself clear. Mr. Collier told a very convincing and straight-forward-seeming story. It may not have been true, but I had reason to believe that it was. I promised him that the matter would be investigated, and that a hearing would be held tomorrow for a final decision. In the light of what I knew at the time, it seemed reasonable to suppose that this request would be granted. However, your story alters the case, naturally. I assure you that California law is anxious to deal fairly and justly. So I hope that you will attend the hearing tomorrow. I will preside, and you can tell your story—and see what he has to say in rebuttal."

"I'll be glad of the chance—and I guess you've got an apology comin', everything considered," Jim said.

"I don't think you've anything to apologize for, Tobey. However, it is only fair to warn you that your story is unsupported, aside from your own word—and that it does have a rather incredible sound."

So long as I know that you're square, I'm not worried about that part of it," Jim assured him. "I'll be there, Governor."

He accompanied the governor to the street again, reassured by the cordiality with which Burnett shook hands, then turned back toward his room.

He stopped suddenly and drew back, almost colliding with someone who was hurrying in the opposite direction. Jim started to mutter a word of apology, checked in amazement. He was looking into the surprised and rather frightened face of the red-head—Alice Osburn.

Twelve

For a moment she looked at him, big-eyed. Then, as she recognized him, her hand, which had gone to her mouth in that old betraying gesture of nervousness, came away. She gave a quick glance about at the covering night, for it was completely dark now. A thin moon was high overhead, the stars were faint and remote. The subdued lights shining through windows, the unsubdued noises of the roistering capital, seemed to make the street itself only that much darker.

"You!" she breathed. "Here!"

"Looks like two of us, and sort of a double surprise," Jim agreed, having recovered himself. "You in any trouble?"

She looked at him quickly, and despite the gloom, he could see the haunting fear in her face—

a sort of desperation which had not been there before. She hesitated, laughed shortly.

"You don't owe me anything," she said. "And I'm not the sort that you'd care to talk to, anyway."

She started to turn away, but Jim frustrated that move. He was sure now that she was in trouble —not the simulated trouble of being thrown off a horse, but real trouble. He drew her arm through his own, turned down toward a quieter street beyond.

"Better tell me about it," he said. "You saved my life for me, and I'm not forgettin' that. Anybody that does that, I figure, is a friend. We're both sort of strangers here, I guess. And you're scairt. You runnin' away from Gold Town—and those others?"

"Yes," she confessed. "They—a friend brought me word. One of them had been drinking, and he swore they were going to find me and kill me. She told me, and I got away. But I—I've just heard that Collier is here—in San Jose. I—I don't know what to do. You've no idea—or maybe you have—the lengths he'll go to."

"I think I've a pretty good notion," Jim assured her. "But he won't know that you're here—not now—and there's a lot of folks around, which kind of helps. Though it might be safer if you headed for some other town tomorrow—San Francisco or Sacramento, or somethin' like that."

"Maybe," she agreed, without much enthusiasm. "I—I have relatives in Monterey."

"Then that's the place for you," Jim said promptly. "You catch the stage out in the morning. Will you?"

"Maybe, she said again. "I don't know."

"What's the trouble?" he asked, divining it. "You broke?"

"Yes," she admitted, looking him full in the face. "It took the last cent I had to get here. I—I was pretty desperate for money, which was why I—why I took that job of Collier's in the first place. I—I'm not quite the sort you probably think I am."

"I never did think nothin' of the kind," Jim assured her promtply. "We all make mistakes now an' then, and I'm comin' to the notion that you're a pretty grand sort of a person. Reckon we can arrange for fare to Monterey all right."

"I'm not begging," she assured him, with a fierceness that matched her red hair. "And you don't owe me anything."

"That's where we don't just see eye to eye," he retorted. "I figure I owe you quite a bit—fact is, I place quite a value on still havin' a whole skin. Nothin' wrong with one friend helpin' another, is there?"

She had stopped again, and was looking at him steadily. What she saw in his face seemed to re-assure her, though her lips trembled for a moment, and she seemed on the verge of tears.

"I—I guess—if you put it that way—"

"That's the way I mean it," Jim said. "And I'll still be a long way in your debt. Likewise, I'll sleep easier if I know you're with friends or rela-tions, and where you belong—and safe from Collier and his crew." He stopped short again. "You have-n't any place to spend the night, have you?"

"I'll make out," she said. "I've done it before."

"But you're not the sort to just make out—and the town's full to overflowin', without a room to be had," he muttered. "I know. I just got hold of a room by luck. You take my room tonight."

He caught the look on her face, went on hastily:

"I'll sleep on the hay in the barn. I've done that before, and in plenty worse places. It won't bother me a bit. You can't do that, of course, but I can.

So you're going to take the room."

She looked at him, and again her eyes seemed about to brim with tears.

"I—I don't deserve anything like that," she said. Jim tucked her arm in his own.

"Things are going to be fine," he assured her. "You just come along, and have a good sleep. I'll tell the clerk how it is, so there won't be no trouble."

The lobby of the hotel was deserted at the moment, except for the clerk who had given him the room. He looked up as they entered. Jim wasted no words.

"I'm givin' this lady my room for the night," he explained. "She just got in town, late, and can't find any place. I'll make out somewhere else."

"Why, shore," the clerk agreed. Such chivalry was understandable enough to him. "That'll be fine."

He went into another room for something or other, leaving them alone. Alice looked at Jim, the light of the lamp reflecting ruddily back from her hair, and again her eyes seemed about to brim.

"I can't find any way to thank you—" she choked. Then suddenly, to his amazement, she kissed him—swiftly, turned as quickly away. "Good night," she whispered, and was climbing the stairs.

Surprised, a little startled even, Jim stared after her, rubbing his chin. Then he went out into the night, crossing the street to the livery barn. He found a bed in the hay without difficulty, and from it, he could look out across the street to the room which he had been expecting to occupy—but which the red-head had now.

It had been an eventful day, and the stage, despite the glowing descriptions of its fast and luxurious travel facilities given in some of the state newspapers, had been dusty and bumpy. He was hardened to such journeys, after the long overland road, but he was tired.

He slept soundly until something roused him. Stirring, he saw that it was just a little past daylight, and San Jose, like Gold Town the day before, was still mostly asleep, after a riotous night. But something, aside from the usual early morning sounds—a horse stomping restlessly in a stall below him, a dog barking on some distant street—had roused him.

This was a second-story room which he had—a haymow above the stable proper, with a window looking out on the street. The windowpane had been removed, so that he had been afforded plenty of fresh air. It was directly opposite, and about on a level with, the room which he had rented in the hotel across the street.

And it was from that room, the window of which stood partly open, that the noise had come which had awakened him. He heard voices, raised in indignation and anger—feminine voices. And both of them were familiar. One belonged to the red-head, which was not surprising. But the other, amazing as it seemed, could belong to only one person. Jeanne!

What was she doing there, when he had supposed that she was a long way off, on the Ranch of the Giants?

"Where is he?" Jeanne's voice was not high pitched, but its very fury lent it a carrying quality. "You—you shameless thing!"

"Who are you, to come breaking into my room?" Alice retorted, equally furious. "I'll call the manager—"

Jim was already tugging his boots on. Since that was all that he had bothered to remove, dressing was a simple matter. He hadn't shaved, and there were a few wisps of hay clinging to him here and there, but he had no time for such trifles. This other thing seemed urgent—more especially as he heard a third voice break in on the argument, a male one, which he judged was probably that of the manager or another clerk.

He had come in through the stable doors and up a ladder, but he took the quicker way now, swinging out of the window, hanging a moment by his hands, then dropping lightly to the ground below. No one seemed to be around to observe this slightly eccentric behavior, but that would not have worried him. He sprinted across the street, and found the door of the hotel unlocked, the lobby empty. He took the stairs two at a time, plunged down the hall. The door was open, the clerk—a different one from the man who had been on duty the night before—standing in the doorway, in the unhappy plight of a man caught between the arguments of two women.

Beyond, inside the room, Jim could see both of them—Jeanne, fully dressed, standing there, and Alice, sitting up in bed.

Jim wasted no time. He barged through the door, shoving the clerk ahead of him before that worthy quite knew what was happening; then he closed the door promptly and, while all three stared at him in astonishment, spoke quickly.

"Let's not wake everybody up," he admonished. "I was sleepin' in the hay, clear across the street, and you woke me up. This can all be explained."

To his surprise, he saw the shadow of a grin cross the red-head's face, and, equally surprising, she remained silent. Jeanne was looking at her with a mixture of emotions, and he saw now that her eyes were red and swollen as if from weeping. But she too was speechless. It was the clerk who spoke, his voice a little acid. Apparently he had just been roused from a sound sleep by the dispute, and was still bewildered and not quite clear in his mind.

"If it can," he said, "I'd like to have somebody do it. I wake up with a row goin' on in this room, at this hour—and this a respectable hotel. And wimmen's voices. But this room was sold to a man. His name's down there on the book. Jim Tobey."

"That's me," Jim explained. "And this girl who's occupyin' it now is an old friend. She came to town last evenin', and couldn't get a room anywhere. So I let her have mine. We explained it to the clerk on duty, so it was all straight. I've been sleepin' in the hay, across there in the barn."

The clerk, and Jeanne as well, gave startled, slowly comprehending glances at the red-head.

"I didn't know about that, but I guess that makes it all right," the clerk agreed. "But what about this other woman? What's she doin', bustin' in here this way, makin' a row? Hey?"

"She's a friend of mine, too, and I have an idea she was looking for me," Jim said. "But you explain that, Jeanne."

Jeanne looked subdued now; the red of anger had faded from her cheeks, leaving them white and drawn. Plainly, she was tired, all used up. Her voice was contrite.

"I am so sorry," she said carefully. "I come to town to find you, yes—and he is snoring in a chair." She nodded a little disgustedly at the clerk. "But the book, eet—it is there, and so I look at it. On it is your name, and the numbair of the room. So, as eet is morning, and I must see you quick—I come up. I knock, and come in. And then—instead of you, here is this woman in bed—I do not understand. I am ver' sorry," she added, turning to Alice.

"I guess we both sort of lost our tempers," Alice said, and flashed a glance at Jim. "Lucky you're always on the job when anything comes up."

The clerk, satisfied, was anxious to be gone. Excusing himself, and with a request that they talk in low tones so as not to disturb the other guests, he went out and closed the door. Jeanne sank wearily into the one chair which the room afforded.

Jim was still amazed at the sight of her.

"What's wrong, Jeanne?" he asked. "Is there trouble back at the ranch?"

"Trobble?" she repeated, and suddenly she was crying again. "There ees nothing else but that, Jeem. They—they come again; they keel the *Señor* and *Señora* and Pedro. Me they try to make prisoner, but I get away. I try to follow you—and in Gold Town someone remembairs that you took the stage yesterday for San Jose, so I ride all night. Oh, Jeem, they have murdaired them—and I had to find you!"

Thirteen

By degrees the story came out. Hank Donney had returned, with some of his cutthroat crew, and this time they had taken the defenders completely by surprise. A fussillade of shots from ambush had killed Gonzales and his wife while they walked, arm in arm, near the house in the cool of the evening.

At least their going had been quick and merciful, and perhaps, in one way, it was the easiest solution for them. They had belonged to a world which had been, but no longer was. One which they had known and enjoyed to the full, but which had passed away when gold had been discovered in the mill race on Sutter's great ranch. None of which excused their killing.

This new world had puzzled them, and they had disliked it intensely because it was harsh and so greatly changed. Now their troubles were over. However, that did not mitigate the enormity of the crime in any way. And the rest of the story made Jim Tobey's eyes cold and hard.

Pedro had appeared, attracted by the gunfire. He had run forward, trying to protect his master and mistress, and had been as coldly shot down. All of this Jeanne had witnessed from where she had been riding, back up the mountain, at the point where Jim had taken her when he circled to watch Donney and Collier.

Margarita, the cook, was an unwilling prisoner, forced to cook for the new crew, but otherwise apparently being treated well enough. They had caught Tony, the stableboy, as well, and had set him to work. And they had lost no time in a general hunt for Jeanne herself, being doubly anxious to make her a captive.

One of them had glimpsed her, and they had ridden in a wild race for miles, but she was mounted on a good horse, and she knew the country better than they did. With night at hand, she had escaped them. Then, stunned by grief, her one thought that she must find Jim in this calamity, she had followed him as well as she could.

Inquiries in Gold Town had been fruitful. Someone remembered seeing a man who answered his description getting on the stage for San Jose. She had kept on, riding most of the night again, had reached the capital and, though she was terrified by the size of the town and the wildness of the thing called civilization, which to her seemed far more savage than the wilderness of the Ranch of the Giants, her desperation had given her a sort of cool courage to overcome any obstacle. Once she could find *Señor* Jeem, everything would be all right— or at least as right as things could ever be again, with the Gonzales gone.

She had left her horse tied, had come there to the City Hotel and been about to make timid inquiries. Then, seeing the open register, and guessing what it was, she had looked at it, rather than disturb the sleeping clerk—partly because she disliked to awaken him unnecessarily, partly because she was timid about talking to strangers when it could be avoided.

And there, sure enough, had been Jim Tobey's name, with the number of his room. Since it was morning already and her need was great, she had stayed for nothing more. She had gone up, tried the door and, finding it unlatched, had timidly pushed it open. Then, when she had found the bed occupied by a strange woman, her pent-up emotions had overflowed in a mingling of anger and despair.

Alice had listened, gradually getting the thing straight in her mind. Now, as Jeanne finished her story and stood blinking back the hot tears, she was suddenly out of the bed and crossing to Jeanne. One arm went comfortingly around her.

"You poor dear!" she said. "And I thought I was having it tough! Those devils!" she added, and her eyes and hair seemed to give off sparks.

"But you've found Jim, and we'll work things out. Here, sit down. Now let's all talk this over."

Jeanne was regaining her composure again now. She had found Jim, and this other girl was a friend. Things were not so dreadful as they had seemed. She even managed a crooked sort of a smile at Alice.

"You are ver' good," she said. "And you have the most beautiful hair I have ever seen."

"That so?" Alice asked. "Glad somebody thinks so. I've been called carrot-top for so long—"

It developed that Jeanne had seen nothing of Bob Reese or the crew which Jim had hired and

141

dispatched to the ranch. What could have happened to them was a little difficult to figure out, but the fact remained that Hank Donney and his crew had struck, and were now in possession.

It was that which puzzled Jim most. He had not expected any such a development—not for a while, at least. Collier had told Donney, in so many words, that he would try other methods first, that nothing like that was to be done; that he did not make war on women. Jim believed that he had been speaking the truth.

And Collier was in the capital now, trying another method which, so far as he could know, promised every chance of success. And however callous Collier might be, he was too polished an adventurer to resort to murder if he could gain his ends by other and legal means.

Also, he was plainly a man who would brook no disobedience on the part of a subordinate, once he had given his orders. It was that which made it so hard to understand. Jim had been sure that there would be no immediate trouble. Yet somewhere, something had gone wrong, and now this had happened.

It need not, he saw, cause any change in his

plans. The real battle for the big ranch was being fought right there in San Jose. If Collier got a new and legal title from the State of California, nothing could oust him. On the other hand, if he was checked in that, he would have no legal leg to stand on, and the ranch could be retaken in due course. Since the Gonzales were past help, and Jeanne was there and safe, a few days made no great difference.

He explained this, recounting his conversation with the governor on the previous evening. Both girls listened with tense interest. Alice nodded her head emphatically.

"In that case," she said, "I'm not taking the stage out this morning. It won't hurt your case to have a couple of witnesses when you talk to him again."

Jim had thought of that, but he had not wanted to suggest it. There were a lot of factors involved. He mentioned one.

"But Collier will find out that you are here, if you do that—and be madder'n ever at you."

Alice tossed her head.

"Let him," she said. "I've a notion that maybe this Governor Peter Burnett is quite a man, and the State of California ought to be able to give me a little protection. Anyway, I owe that hombre something—and this may be a chance to pay it back."

Jeanne was looking from one to the other, wide-eyed.

"But what ees this?" she asked. "Weeth you and Collier?"

Color stained Alice's cheeks for a moment.

"It's not a pretty story," she said. "But likely you'll have to hear it anyway, so I might as well be the one to tell you. I reckon you'll despise me then—even if Jim has forgiven me. But you run along now, Jim, and find her horse and stable it. Give us a chance to freshen up a little, and then—if you still want to go with me, after everything—we'll all go out and have some breakfast."

Jim did as suggested, found the horse and cared for it. He made arrangements with the clerk to borrow a razor, and felt considerably more presentable when he had used it. Since he was going to have a hearing before the governor, and in the presence of a couple of beautiful girls, he didn't want to look too much like a backwoodsman.

The girls, too, had undergone a transformation. Jeanne had been tired and dirty from her long trip, but she looked fresh and neat now, and it was apparent that she had listened with a sympathetic ear to Alice's confession. The two seemed now to be fast friends.

Jim smiled a little to himself. Collier, expecting that everything was settled except for legal formalities, was going to be in for a nasty shock when he found himself confronted by three witnesses who could tell such a damning story against him.

Today, there was a certain amount of formality. A clerk took their names and admitted them to a pleasant room where a long table stood, surrounded by several comfortable chairs. Governor Burnett was seated at the head of the table, and a clerk was at one side, with several sheets of paper. Collier, impeccably dressed and freshly shaven, lounged by a window, smoking a cigar. He turned slowly as they entered, then stared, frozen. Plainly, the governor had not told him that anything new had developed, a fact confirmed by the sly smile on Burnett's long face.

Now the governor was on his feet, bowing to the ladies, his eyebrows slightly elevated as he glanced at Jim. Jim bowed low in return.

"Governor," he said, "allow me to present two

most important witnesses in this case—Miss Jeanne, adopted daughter of the Gonzales, and Miss Alice Osburn, that I was tellin' you about last night."

The governor's manners were perfect, despite his obvious surprise. And by now, Collier was mastering his own. His face was controlled again, though there was an uneasiness in his eyes which he could not quite hide. This hearing was not going to be the triumphant formality to which he had looked forward.

"I believe that you are all acquainted with each other," Burnett said, his voice a little cold, looking at Collier.

Collier shrugged, and bowed to Jeanne.

"I have met this charming lady once," he acknowledged.

"And you send your hoodlums to murder the *Señor* and *Señora*," Jeanne flashed. "And still you pose as the gentleman!"

Astonishment showed for a moment on Collier's face. He seemed quite unaware of the governor's sudden sharp glance at him.

"Murder?" he repeated. "I'm afraid I don't know what you mean."

"What she means," Jim said coldly, "is that

146

Hank Donney and his crew, whom you turned loose instead of taking them to the law as you promised to do, returned and murdered the Gonzales, shooting them down from ambush before her very eyes. They also killed Pedro, and did their best to capture Jeanne. She managed to escape by hard riding, and set out to find me—and as luck would have, did so, this mornin'."

As Jim had observed before, Collier was a gambler, long schooled in presenting an expressionless face to the world, a mask for his real emotions. But now he showed a lively interest that, it seemed to Jim, must be genuine. There was a moment of fury, before he mastered himself, and shock and horror also showed in his eyes.

Jim decided that he had come on down to San Jose to attend to the vital matter of the title to the big ranch. That was the thing of paramount importance, as Collier knew well enough.

But while doing that, he had left Donney and the rest of his crew to wait for further orders, and Donney, chafing at the restraint imposed on him, angry at the sarcasm with which Collier had greeted his failure to get control of the ranch, had been in just the mood to show his boss that he

147

could do things in his own way. And he had probably been driven by the desire to make Jeanne a
captive, with no one like Collier around to restrain
him.

So he had returned to the ranch, had brutally
carried out his own plan, not even exercising the
degree of restraint which had spoiled his first attempt. But all this, Jim guessed, had been without
Collier's knowledge or authorization, and he was
both dismayed and furious at what such murderous
bungling had done to his plans.

Collier shook his head now, his voice tight.

"Believe me," he said, "this is all news to me.
News which, I assure you, I exceedingly regret."

The governor's face had gone cold. He turned
to Jeanne, asked her a few searching but sympathetic questions. It was plain to see that, if he had
not quite accepted Jim's story the evening before,
any lingering doubts had been removed now.

Collier, it was equally plain, was thinking fast.
That morning he had been completely certain of
victory. Now he was shrewd enough to know that
his last chance in that direction was gone, ruined
by his hireling's bungling. If nothing had happened
at the Ranch of the Giants, and Hank Donney had

kept out of sight, so that he could deny any story which Jim might tell, he might have brazened out the hearing with some chance of success.

Now it was impossible, and if he submitted to questioning before those witnesses, he would not only gain nothing, but might find himself convicted and under arrest for complicity in some of the murder attempts. But again, since he was a gambler, his face betrayed nothing of that. He bowed very formally to the governor.

"Apparently things are not to be so simple as I had anticipated," he said. "I find myself opposed by three witnesses. So I think it only fair that you allow me to bring certain witnesses of my own, by which I may be able to prove my case, and also to refute some of the charges which seem to be lodged against me. If you'll postpone the hearing for half an hour, I'll have three of them here."

The governor hesitated, then agreed. After all, no charges of a criminal nature had so far been lodged against Collier—at least not in a legal manner. This was a scheduled hearing, and that was Collier's right. Collier bowed briefly to all of them.

"In half an hour," he promised, and walked unhurriedly from the room.

Fourteen

Even when he was out of the building, Collier did not appreciably increase his pace. His impulse was to take to his heels; he was fearful that at any moment the governor would regret his permission and send someone to fetch him back. Collier's hand slid inside his coat pocket. Anyone who tried it would have a job on his hands.

He had lost, in the big gamble for title to the ranch; lost just when success had seemed to be in his grasp. But he did not waste a second thought on that. It would have been a rich piece of booty, and would have greatly simplified matters in other ways, but spilled milk was gone, and there were other high stakes left to play for. The thing now was to get out of town before he was stopped.

An excellent-looking cayuse, saddled and ready and champing at the bit, was at a convenient hitching post. With the building between himself and possible observation by the governor or Jim and the two girls, Collier walked, still unhurriedly, to the horse, untied it, vaulted into the saddle, and rode away. He was tense until he had rounded the corner, but no owner appeared to shout after him, and he promptly put the animal to a gallop.

He had some luggage, including a purse with a good bit of money in it, in a hotel room. But he dared not lose valuable time in going after it now. His destination, just as soon as he could get there, was the Ranch of the Giants.

In the first place, he had a score to settle with Hank Donney. Though few would have guessed it, there was a soft spot somewhere deep in Collier's heart, which the hard crust had not quite covered. He had liked Gonzales and his charming lady, and he sincerely regretted what had happened to them. That had been no part of his plan. Too, he had liked Jeanne, that beautiful, fresh, unspoiled child of nature, and he regretted even more sincerely the grief and danger to which she had been subjected.

He had even toyed with the notion, once the title to the ranch was in his hands, of leaving the Gonzales there as before, and not bothering to tell them that he was the real owner. After all, they were old, pleasant, and harmless. And if he made a good impression on them, that would almost certainly put him in Jeanne's good graces.

Now those plans were spoiled, and needlessly, and fury was strong in him. Hank Donney had gone too far. That was one imperative reason for getting back to the ranch before anyone could stop him. He had a score to settle with Donney.

And, all sentiment aside, there was still work to do. Work which, he was convinced now, could best be handled from the Ranch of the Giants.

Out of town, he rode fast, not sparing the horse. It would be easy to pick up other horses along the road, in the same manner. And he knew with certainty that Jim Tobey would soon be coming that way, back to the ranch. That was the way he wanted it. Only it was imperative that he be there first.

Showdown between Jim and himself was inevitable. That didn't worry him. It was what he wanted. Jim Tobey's luck couldn't last forever. Every string had a break in it somewhere sooner or later. When that time came, he'd get hold of the silver cayuse.

Hope brightened the gambler's eyes as he thought of it. That had been a piece of real luck, finding the man who wore such a ring.

He had wondered at first where and how Jim could have gotten hold of it. Though the really important thing had been to get hold of it for himself. The fool had refused to sell it, and Collier's tries at getting it hadn't worked—but he'd win it yet.

He had things pretty well fitted together in his mind now. The girl, of course. Jeanne. She had been an orphan, taken in by the Gonzales. Raised by them. And she had lost her parents while she was still very young, somewhere in the country near *El Gianto*. Killed, supposedly, by Indians.

None of that had seemed important or even particularly interesting when he had first gleaned those crumbs of facts. Now it was very much to the point. Collier was reasonably certain that Indians had been blamed for a crime of which they were innocent. Jeanne's father had been murdered so that somebody could obtain possession of that ring, for he must have been the owner of it. And his wife had been killed because she fought beside her man.

But because a baby had been playing with the ring, the killers had failed to get it. And, unsuspecting its real value, Jeanne had evidently cherished it all these years; then, because it did mean so much to her, she had turned it over to Jim, for him to wear as a sort of favor or talisman. Collier was reasonably certain that this was the real explanation.

The Gonzales, of course, must have known that Jeanne had the ring. Whether they had realized its true significance or not was hard to tell. Most probably not. In any case, they had said nothing about it, done nothing. That would undoubtedly mean that Gonzales had been ignorant of what it meant.

Collier was reasonably sure of his facts. His mind went back down the years. He had been a wild young hellion when he had been in California many years before. Only fourteen when he had first run away to sea. The black sheep of an otherwise highly respectable family.

When he had deserted ship and landed in California, there had been a double reason behind it. First, he had had more than enough of seafaring, of the stern discipline of shipboard and all the rest of it. California, by all reports, was a sleepy, mellow land, and it would be pleasant to visit it, to do as he pleased.

That had been one reason. The other had been more vital. Piracy on the high seas had pretty well been stamped out, though it was far from dead. But there were many degrees and methods of piracy, particularly in some of the fabulous lands of the East where the ship had touched—sometimes remaining for weeks at a time.

Collier had found it far more profitable to turn his hand to certain aspects of this than to work entirely as a sailor at deck hand's pay. It had been his plan to jump ship at one of these eastern ports, but certain events had made it necessary, even desirable, to sail with his ship again. In fact, he'd been glad that it was sailing then, and not even twenty-four hours later.

There had been a matter of some blood-spilling, of jewels worth a king's ransom—the jewels, incidentally, being on board ship when it made sail.

It had been a keen, though rare enough pleasure, for Collier and a couple of confederates to run their fingers through that loot when opportunity offered. Here were pearls to grace the throat of a favorite of the Sultan. Diamonds that rippled like liquid fire. Emeralds, some of which had served once as eyes for heathen deities. Opals, rubies—

Collier's eyes brightened at the memory. That had been one reason he had considered deserting. The captain had gotten wind of some of these activities, and was resolved to find out what was going on, what loot was hidden on his vessel, if any, and who was involved. Since he was a harsh man and a just, the punishments which he meted out still made Collier's flesh crawl, even in retrospection.

He had deserted, along with his two shipmates—with that fabulous loot. One of the two had died, short of shore, a musket-ball from the captain's gun through his skull. He had been swimming with the bag clutched in one hand, but Collier had been quick enough to grab it and save it.

On shore, well heeled, he had soon learned about the outlaws who were terrorizing the country. There were a few natives, sons of rich land owners, black sheep. But for the most part they were adventurers like himself, deserters from hell ships. It had been a natural thing to join the organization, to assume a leading position in it.

There had been a few wild months. Desperate

forays, interspersed with days or weeks of idleness, of pleasant living. Shy young *señoritas*, with eyes soft and bright by moonlight. True, they had been guarded by duennas who were worse than the scimitar-wielding sentries set about a Turk's harem, but even they could be outwitted, and it all added to the thrill of the game. Collier sighed a little, remembering.

Then had come the outraged action of substantial citizens, who had formed themselves into the Committee of Twenty, the insignia of which was the silver cayuse. Not many of them—only a score. Less than a third as many as those who preyed upon the hitherto helpless countryside. For the law had been a thing to laugh at.

But those twenty, including one Gringo, had been as bold and desperate as any of their enemies. And determined. How they had done it was still some matter of wonder in Collier's mind, but they had broken up the gang, shooting some, running others through with swords, hanging a full dozen. From a fair haven, an apple ripe for the plucking, California had suddenly become a highly dangerous place.

In these counter-forays, the Committee of

Twenty had found much of the loot of which they and others had been robbed, as well as a good portion of the booty brought by various outlaws when they had set foot on California's soil—such booty as that which had been in Collier's own hand when he crawled ashore that first night. They had stumbled upon the gang's headquarters, and lesser quarters as well. And they had found imperishable treasure, such as pearls, diamonds, rubies, gold, to the value of at least a million and a half dollars.

Collier, one of the few members of the gang remaining alive and at large at the time, had been acutely aware of that fact. He had been desperately anxious to get on to some ship—any ship that happened to put in, if he could manage it—and get out of that buzzing hornet's nest before he was caught and stung to death. But he had hated the thought of going more empty-handed than he had come.

Being more boldly venturesome than most, he had not only been successful, but had kept alive, up to then. Venturing again, he had learned a secret of import. The Committee of Twenty—or those of it who still remained alive, for they too, had suffered losses, and had not taken any new recruits— had been too busy for a time cleaning up the outlaws to bother much with lesser details. Likewise, most of the loot had been recovered only recently.

Now, with the lawless gang pretty well broken up or killed off, they had turned their attention to the matter of finding the rightful owners of the treasure trove, so that it could be returned to those owners. Not an easy matter, when much of it was jewels or gold, and unmarked.

Their intentions had been strictly honest. But, moving in secret as they had been compelled to do to work successfully, they had hidden the loot—if reports were accurate, and Collier believed that they had been—all in one spot.

There they had agreed to gather upon a certain date, every man of the Committee who remained alive, to take it and decide upon its disposition.

They moved secretly, often masked, frequently not disclosing their identities even to one another, save by the secret code of the silver cayuse, and this hiding of the treasure had been done in the same manner, by one or two members. Collier knew that. And the secret of the hiding place had been as carefully kept—in one or two of the rings.

Collier had become familiar with those dread

rings. And he, alone of all his gang, so he believed, had finally learned their secret. The rearing cayuse of solid silver wrought upon the ring concealed a clever catch, which in turn had a small opening inside.

In that, a small bit of paper with a message upon it could be hidden. And one or more of the rings had the secret of the cache!

Excitement had filled him then, when he had learned that the remaining members of the Committee were to gather with all the booty for division or distribution. He had laid his plans so that he might leave California, and not empty-handed.

But fate, or luck, had intervened again. Sudden sickness had fatally stricken two of the remaining Committee men. And the member's of Collier's own reorganizade gang, whom he had dispatched to get hold of one of the few remaining rings, which might hold the secret of the cache—they had failed. There near the Ranch of the Giants.

Jeanne's parents had died—indirectly, at least, by his order. And to no profit. Always since then he had blamed himself for not being along at the time.

So far as he had been able to learn back in those

days, retribution had overtaken every remaining member of the dread Committee of Twenty—there had been only a scant handful. Retribution in the form of sickness, or a fall from a horse, or in some other guise. At least he had called it retribution.

But the devil of it was that they had died, the silver cayuses had vanished, and with them had gone the secret, so badly wanted by men on both sides, of where that treasure had been hidden.

There had still been other men, not of the original Committee, to make things hot. California had become impossible. He had been lucky to get away —without even a cent of that treasure which he had helped to garner.

Now he had returned, drawn by a double lure of gold. No longer would he be known or sought by the law. And he had pieced a few facts carefully together over the years. If he was right in his deductions and guesses, that treasure trove must be on or near the remote Ranch of the Giants—which had explained his interest in it.

The Gringo had had a beautiful Spanish wife. So Jeanne was probably wrong in supposing her mother to have been American too. And if he was right in other things, then the secret was hidden in that silver cayuse which rode Jim Tobey's finger. So it was very well that Tobey should come seeking him at the big ranch.

Fifteen

Outwardly, there was little change in the Ranch of the Giants since Collier had seen it last. It was still so remote that the flood tide of gold seekers had scarcely ebbed that far, and the big trees on the hills lifted serene branches to the sun. All was very peaceful. But Collier was too old a hand to go rushing in.

Hank Donney had acted without his orders, or rather in defiance of them. What the man might have in mind was a thing to be discovered. Collier had long since made sure that there is no honor among thieves.

It was just past sunset when he approached the building, keeping well hidden in the brush, and not following the road. A quarter of a mile away, he left his horse and proceeded on foot. And, having·reached a vantage-point not far from the house, he stayed where he could see without being seen when the others came sauntering outside after supper.

There was a watchful air about them, Collier noted, as though they were well aware that they could sooner or later expect trouble. But Donney himself walked with a swagger, picking his teeth with the point of a bowie knife.

"We're settin' pretty," he said. "Right on top uh the world—and we're going to keep on doing it. Collier figgered there'd be more money in ranchin' than in huntin' for gold, and I reckon he's right. Only we ain't turnin' this place over to him. We took it, and it's a case of finders keepers."

"What'll you tell him when he shows up?" someone demanded.

Donney grinned unpleasantly.

"When he shows up," he said, "we'll give him what he wants—a piece of the Giant. A chunk of land he can have permanent. With the sod in his face. I won't begrudge him that much, for givin' me the idea in the first place."

Collier heard this without surprise. He fingered the gun at his hip, considering. It was a remote country, and he was an excellent shot. He could kill Donney as he stood, and he had little doubt but that the rest of them would fall readily enough in line again and obey his orders. But he did not lift the gun from leather.

Something might go wrong, with night so close at hand. And there was no need to take chances, when Donney, alive, might be useful. If his guess was correct, Jim Tobey would be arriving before long, probably with a crew behind him. Let them deal with Donney—and Donney with them. After that, he would make his move.

"Plainly, he's not coming back," the governor said a little grimly. "Which seems to establish him as the scoundrel you have painted him. But it also establishes your claim—or that of Miss Jeanne—to the ranch. For if the Gonzales are dead, I suppose that she is their heir?"

"It seems that way to me," Jim agreed.

Governor Burnett stroked his long chin for a moment.

"Of course, from a legal standpoint, all of this is rather irregular," he pointed out. "Though a lot of things have been that way in this country for some time. Proof of their death, and of their original ownership of the land, all enter in. There is always the possibility of other heirs, possible relatives, putting in a claim. So naturally, no final disposition can be made at this time.

"But I assure you that no one else will be allowed to gain a legal hold on the ranch without your claims being heard and given full consideration. And in the meantime, we'll go on the assumption that Miss Jeanne is the legal heir, and you will continue to act as foreman, in charge of things. Is that satisfactory?"

"Havin' your word on it is all we wanted," Jim assured him. "And now, since Collier can't cause any more trouble here, reckon we'll be startin' back for the ranch."

Outside, he stopped, looking from Jeanne to Alice and back again.

"First off, we'd better see about getting you on the stage for Monterey," he said, "so you'll be all right."

Decisively, Alice shook her head.

"I'd rather go along with the two of you, if you don't mind," she said. "I'm in this now, and I'd like to see the finish of it. Besides, I don't suppose that such relatives as I have in Monterey would be overjoyed to see me. I can sort of act as a chaperone on the trip—not that you need any, of course." Her eyes were dancing; then she sobered.

"And the way it looks to me, you'll probably run into trouble when you get there. As it happens, I can use a gun about as well as a man. I had to, a few times, coming West in a covered wagon. I might be useful."

Jeanne approved. The two girls, after the initial misunderstanding, seemed to have taken strongly to each other. There was nothing for Jim to do but agree. He suggested that they wait until the next morning, to give Jeanne a chance to rest up a bit, since she had been riding almost night and day since leaving the ranch. The argument which won his point was that she would have to leave her favorite horse behind, unless it could have the chance to rest up.

Despite her trip, and her grief for her foster-parents, Jeanne was too excited to waste all of her precious time in sleeping. She did sleep for a few hours, then insisted on seeing the town with them. The teeming capital was a new experience to her, who had scarcely set foot off the ranch until this trip. But when, the next morning, the three of them rode out of town, she shoot her head soberly.

"It was ver' interesting," she said. "But I do not like it—not for long. I would not weesh to live in such a great city."

She had re-examined the silver cayuse with considerably interest, after Jim explained Collier's and the governor's interest in it. But she insisted that he continue to wear it.

"I think eet is good luck, Jeem," she said. "So I want you to have it."

It was the afternoon of the second day on the road that they encountered Bob Reese and the crew which Jim had dispatched, days before, toward the big ranch. Reese looker both relieved and sheepish at sight of him.

"We sure ain't been carryin' out your orders," he said. "Though it ain't been for the lack o' tryin'. We got kind of lost up here 'n the hills. Asked a feller for directions, and he told us where to go. He was a big feller, with a lot of whiskers, and he sure enough lied to us. Got us way off in the wrong direction, and we wandered around for days tryin' to get to somewhere."

"Sounds like you ran into Hank Donney himself," Jim said. This explained the failure of his men to show up; if they had, it might have made a big difference in the fortunes of the Gonzales. But the thing had happened, and there was nothing that could be done about it. On being told what had happened at the ranch, the crew were grim. If there was a fight ahead, they were in just the mood for it now.

That there would be a fight, Jim had not the least doubt. Donney would not lightly give up what he had already done murder for. And by now, Collier would be there, too.

With such a force at his heels, Jim rode rapidly, not stealthily, as Collier had done. Again it was a pleasant afternoon, verging on evening, and everything had an ageless, peaceful look. A spiral of smoke arose lazily from the chimney of the house, visible from a considerable distance down the road. And then, from a brushy turn of it, a voice challenged him.

"You've come far enough! Pull up, thar!"

The order was emphasized a moment later by the thunderous blast of a gun fired over their heads. That was meant partly as a warning, of course, partly as a signal to the others on the ranch that they had arrived, so that reinforcements could come.

The shot was a mistake. Reese's temper was short, after the way he had been put upon, and the noise of the gun betrayed its whereabouts to his keen eyes. He jerked a revolver and sent back a couple of shots in quick tempo, and that was all that was needed. The brush was not thick enough to stop bullets. It jerked, as a heavy body thrashed in it, and that was all.

Recklessly enough, Reese spurred ahead, but in this case it was safe. The guard who had been posted there had sounded the warning, but he was past doing it again or halting any advance on their part. However, Jim held up his hand.

"Looks like he was alone, right here," he said. "But the rest of them will be on the watch. So we'll leave the road and circle—and watch your step, now! They'll shoot to kill next time, without warning."

As a further precaution, he sent half of them to the right, the rest to the left. That way, they would approach the buildings from opposite directions, and their own danger would be lessened. The girls went with him, as well as a couple of the men.

"Eet—it was awful, the way he was there, in his own blood," Jeanne whispered, as they picked a cautious way ahead. She shivered a little. "But it was what he deserved. It was he who shot the *Señora*. I saw him do it."

"In that case, he sure got what was comin' to him," Jim agreed. This was a bad business, not at all to his liking. He had come to that remote section of country looking for peace, but there were too many reckless men, scum swept off the backwash of the world, who had landed in California. Governor Burnett had spoken of a vigilance society, the wearers of the silver cayuse. They had smashed one wave of lawlessness, a score or so of years ago. It would take something on the same order, probably, to bring law and peace to California again.

Meanwhile, like it or not, force had to be met with force. There was no other way.

The sun had set, and the shadows were claiming the land. There had been no more shooting, no other challenge. But it was plain that the trespassers were alert, and undoubtedly on guard at the buildings. They circled, making their way through a stand of tall pine trees, the heavy, fragrant carpeting of needles a silent cushion underfoot. Jeanne suddenly gave a stifled exclamation.

Following her gaze, Jim understood. There were three new-made graves.

There was no mark of identification upon them, but there could be little doubt as to who was buried there. They went on again, more cautiously now, and someone called from the closing dark ahead. Bob Reese's voice.

Jim answered, and Reese joined them.

"They're there, all right," he reported. "What do we do? Rush'm from both sides?"

Out of the thickening gloom, the sardonic voice of Hank Donney came in answer.

"Come right ahead—if you want to try it. We're ready for yuh—ready an' anxious."

Since there was nothing to shoot back at this time, Reese merely fumed. Donney spoke again.

"We got possession here, an' we're keepin' it. Don't make no mistake about that."

"We'll mighty soon root you out'n there, when we come," Reese yelled, infuriated.

Donney's answer was a dry chuckle.

"Hogs root," he said. "But there's somethin' else yuh might like to know. We got that fat Mexican cook here, quackin' like a dish uh jelly. An' if there's a rush, first thing we do's to put a bullet right through her. Tell that to the gal!"

Beside him, Jim heard the quick catch of Jeanne's breath. She spoke passionately.

"Oh, Jeem, we cannot risk that! Margarita, she has always been so good—my nurse, and all. No, no, that weel not do."

"Don't worry, we're in no hurry," Jim reassured her. "The strain's on them, not us. We can get along just as well out here tonight as if we had the house again. They're the ones that'll lose sleep."

Then, raising his voice, he called back:

"We won't be makin' any attack—not just now, Donney. But don't go makin' any mistakes like you just mentioned. If anything like that happens to the cook, we'll take you alive, then cut your ears off before we string you up. Just keep it in mind."

Donney retorted with fresh and abusive threats, but Jim knew that he would be sufficiently impressed to think twice before harming any hostage. The man was a coward at heart, as he had shown when Collier had taunted him on his failure the first time.

Leaving a guard to keep watch on the buildings, the rest of them quietly withdraw for some distance to the shelter of a canyon. Down in there they could have a cook fire and camp securely. And as Jim had pointed out, there was no great hurry. Time was on their side. And the strain of waiting, constantly on guard, would wear thin the nerves of the others.

Sixteen

The night was quiet enough. The initiative now lay with Jim, and he was in no hurry to press for a showdown.

Back here on *El Gianto*, Jeanne, though still depressed by her grief, seemed more contented than she had been. And the red-head was joking and bantering with Reese as the two of them cooked breakfast. When he went down to a small creek to dip up a pail of water, stepping out on an old log, she slyly joggled the log, sending him headlong into the icy waters.

He came up, splashing and blowing, but grinning. Alice screamed as he reached the shore, and started, too late, to flee. He caught her, carried her back, kicking and struggling, swung her as if about to fling her out to the middle of the creek, then, still laughing, set her down on dry ground.

"I sure ought to throw you in an' cool that red head o' your'n," he said. "But I ain't had so much fun since I left Ohio, so I guess I'll let you off this time."

"Let me off!" Alice spluttered. "You've got me just about as wet as you are yourself! Look at me!"

"I am," Reese grinned. "Look right purty, too. Makes yore cheeks match your hair. And if I'm sorter damp you know how I got that way."

"Those two," Jeanne pronounced, watching them, "they like each other, a lot."

"Guess we better take over breakfast," Jim suggested. "They'll let it burn, 'fore they remember about it."

Breakfast over, he saddled his horse again. This would be a good time to look things over more thoroughly than he had been able to do before. He wanted to know more about the big ranch, the better to plan what would have to be done. A day or so of delay in getting possession of the buildings did not matter.

But very soon now, the strayed herds must be rounded up, the hay cut and stacked, a lot of jobs done before snow came. It would be a close race with time, but he had to know the place better before he could plan efficiently.

Aside from the buildings, the ranch was in their control again. Jim saw occasional scattered bunches of cattle, more than half wild. None of the younger stock had ever been branded. The pasture was excellent, however, and the fields which in other years had been cut for hay were tall with it now. It was over-ripe, but it would be better than nothing; with the old hay-stacks, it would carry them through the winter.

Here were open fields, with thick forests flanking them. Dim, cathedral-like aisles ran between mighty trees, some of which had been tall when Columbus dreamed. Riding among these, he came out upon an open section of several acres, with a sharply rising hill in the background. Here were a lot of boulders, scattered haphazardly, some as big as small houses.

But it was not those which caught his attention now. Standing squarely in front of the hill, two pinnacles of rock reared skyward. They were at least twenty feet thick at the base, not quite so big at the top, though very nearly. Both were almost square, and they rose up for seventy feet or more.

They were odd, striking in appearance—curious manifestations of nature in a prodigal mood. And then a sudden thought struck him.

"These must be the Giants," he muttered. "Likely they're what the ranch was named after in the first place."

But big pinnacles of rock, however odd they might be, were incidental to the business of getting a big ranch to running again. He swung off to one side, into deeper timber again, then stopped as his cayuse snorted and seemed reluctant to go ahead.

The reason was easy to understood. In the soft leafy mold just ahead were the tracks of a bear—and these had been made by no ordinary bear. A grizzly had traveled along there, and a big one. But it had probably been gone for several hours, and these days, when they were normally well fed and sleepy, there was not much danger. Yet, as Jim well knew, a grizzly was an unpredictable sort of a critter at best, and you could never be quite sure when one might take a notion to start something.

But the trail didn't look fresh to him. Likewise, it seemed that the bear had lost a couple of toes on one front foot at some time or other. He dismounted for a better luck, for such things were always full of keen interest for him. He was bending over when a sudden sense of danger warned him.

Brush grew close on one side. And it was possible that the bear might be lurking thereabouts still, since Jim's horse was again showing signs of nervousness. He started to straighten, and in that instant he saw it coming—something like a huge paw, striking at him from the brush. Only it was not a paw. It was a club, smashing down at his skull.

More by instinct than anything else, he managed to fling himself partly to the side, twisting a little. Enough to save his life, to keep the club from crushing his head as though it had been a tinsel toy. But not quite enough to avoid the blow altogether.

It caught him as he came partly up, sent him flat on hands and knees again, and so down full length on to the leafy mold. A red-shot blackness seemed to explode in his head, and as he pitched forward, his last conscious thought was that this was the end. That club was in the hand of Hank Donney, and if the one stroke hadn't been enough, he'd finish the job.

Something was biting at his finger. That was his first disjointed impression. Then, as his head cleared a little and he could think again, Jim realized that something was tugging at the ring on his finger—the silver cayuse. It fit a bit snugly and wasn't coming off easily.

Instinctively, he tried to clench his fist, but now the ring had come off and his hand was allowed to drop. His head was still a bit befuddled, aching from the blow that he had taken, but now he could think again. And he had an impression that he had not been unconscious very long—not more than a couple of minutes or so.

His muscles were still not quite ready to respond to his will, so that it was hard even to pry open his eyes. But with them open, he could see, and he stared in increasing bewilderment.

It was Collier who had pulled the ring off his finger. He stood now a few paces away, examining it with a lively interest, a pleased smile on his face. And then Jim saw something else, which chilled him like a cold wind.

Lying almost at his feet, sprawled in a spreading pool of his own blood, was Hank Donney. The blood still ran from a gunshot wound just above the heart.

He must have made some sound, for Collier's

eyes jerked from the ring in his hand back to Jim, sharpening intently. Then, seeing how sick and dazed Jim still was, they grew passive again, rather like the hooded eyes of a hawk.

"Still alive, are you, Tobey?" he asked. "I rather thought he'd smashed your skull for you—but you're a hard-headed cuss, aren't you?"

Jim did not reply. As his head cleared, understanding came with it. He had been in a tight spot a few minutes before, and it seemed that Collier, for purposes of his own, had saved his life for him —though that had been purely incidental, a side issue to his main purpose. The thing which counted was that Collier had just killed a man in cold blood.

"I've been keeping an eye on you ever since you started out this morning," Collier explained. "I aimed to get this ring, when the proper chance offered. Then, a little while ago, I discovered that Donney was trailing you, too—his notion being, I presume, that if he could slip away and trail you and kill you, he'd have a lot less trouble on his hands."

Collier held the ring to the light, squinted with satisfaction at the silver cayuse, rubbed it on his sleeve for a moment, and went on, without turning his head.

"I took care, of course, that neither of you should discover me. And when he saw what you were going to do—take a look at the bear tracks—and got around ahead of you, it was simple enough for him—with you off your horse. But it rather turned sour in his mouth, I think, when he saw me coming up. And before he could drop his club and grab for his gun, I shot him. And, without intending it that way, it appears that I saved your life for you."

Still Jim said nothing. Strength was beginning to flow back into him again as the effects of the blow wore off, but he knew what he was up against now. Collier had, probably out of old habit, helped himself to Jim's gun at the same time that he took the ring. Jim could see it stuck in his belt now. And though Donney had had a gun, too, it was too far off for him to stand much chance of getting it.

His only chance lay in making Collier believe that he was still dazed and helpless. That way, he would postpone the inevitable, and when he got his strength back, he might have a fighting chance.

"Since you're still alive," Collier went on, "I'll have to finish what he started, of course. You've gotten in my way too many times. He only did it once—but even once is too many, with me."

He flicked another of those gimlet glances at Jim, seemed satisfied, and went on with his inspection of the ring.

"As I suppose you have gathered, I'm really quite interested in this silver cayuse. I knew that I'd get it, sooner or later. Ah!"

Something had excited his keener interest. Now, as Jim stirred a little, Collier darted a sharp look at him, and one hand dropped to his holster and came up with a smooth motion, his revolver clutched in it.

"Since you're starting to get back to normal, I'll have to finish you off," he added, as casually as if speaking of the time of day. Still watching Jim, he took a side step or two, laying the ring down on top of a stone which stood there—a small boulder, three or four feet high. The sun caught the polished silver of it and reflected back.

"It's much too valuable to take any chances with," Collier explained. "And if you're curious, I might say that I've just succeeded in getting the little catch open—a highly ingenious arrangement, worked by one of the front paws of the cayuse. And inside, as I had hoped, seems to be a message which has been there for a good many years. I don't want to risk being disturbed when I read it, so—"

He glanced very swiftly at the ring, to make sure that it would not roll off. In that instant, the gun barrel wavered a trifle, for he was still convinced that Jim was groggy. Jim had waited, hoping for a more favorable opportunity. Collier might come closer, for instance.

But it was now or never. He tensed, gathering himself for a leap, and one hand, digging in the leafy mold at his side, came up with a handful of it. Even as he raised up, Jim flung it full in Collier's face. The gun blasted at almost the same instant.

Surprise was on Jim's side, however, and the dirt, hitting him in the face, spoiled Collier's aim. Then he was clawing at his face with one hand, temporarily blinded, and the next instant Jim was on top of him.

His rush bowled Collier over, onto the ground. Then they were struggling frenziedly for possession of the gun. He had battled Collier a few

nights before in the heavy blackness of his bed-
room, and each man knew that in the other they
had a formidable opponent. And both knew that
this was for keeps.

Jim wanted to get hold of that gun, but his first
thought was to keep Collier from using it. In that,
at least, he was successful. The gun was knocked
from Collier's hand as he hit the ground and rolled,
and for the moment, at least, neither of them could
get hold of it.

Even while he struggled to hold Jim off, Collier
was slapping with one hand, trying to get hold of
Jim's gun, which he had stuck in his belt. Frustration, anger and amazement showed in his face as
he fumbled unsuccessfully. Then it was borne in
upon him, as upon Jim, that the second gun, too,
had slipped and fallen when Collier had hit the
ground so hard.

That left them to fight on even terms. Convinced that he had no choice, Collier was bending
every energy to ending it as quickly as possible.
He still believed that Jim was more than half
groggy, not in much shape for a fight.

In that, he was at least partly right. Jim's head
still ached, his strength was not fully back. But he

was in reasonably good shake, and he had no intention of losing this fight. Too much was at stake —including his own life.

Somewhere in the nearby tree tops, a bird watched them and screamed raucously, excitedly. Insects hummed near them, faintly disturbed by what went on. Neither man noticed.

Locked together, they were rolling around on the ground, and Collier was without scruple when it came to fighting. Moreover, in his varied career, he seemed to have picked up all the tricks that anyone had ever heard of or used, and the veneer of late years had not caused him to forget. Jim found himself hard put to evade some of his opponent's more murderous attempts. But his own education had been pretty well rounded out in the last wild year or so.

He grabbed a handful of hair, jerked Collier's head up and thumped it back on the ground, hard. All that saved Collier was that the ground at that spot was soft and loamy.

It was a dog fight now. It seemed to Jim that it had been going on endlessly, and he knew that, discounting his weakness, it must actually have been quite a while. His shirt was half torn from his back,

Collier's coat was in ribbons. Both of them were gasping for breath, both weakening, but the advantage lay this time with Collier.

Remembering what had happened before, he had managed to keep Jim's fingers off his throat, and that blow of the club was taking its toll of Jim's strength now. He had to do something soon, he knew, or he was finished. And it seemed impossible even to lift his arm again, let alone to manage anything decisive.

Seventeen

He had heard no sound, above the noise of their own scuffling and hoarse gasping for breath. But perhaps there had been something else, like a whiff of heavy scent. Collier had manager to get uppermost, winning a slow advantage. Now he raised his head suddenly and stared at something which Jim could not see, and his face went blank with astonishment and a little loose.

For a moment he stared, and the pasty white of fright was added to the looseness in his face. Moving so fast that it left Jim bewildered, he scrambled to his feet and began running, all in an instant. From being on the verge of exhaustion he seemed all at once imbued with a vast flood of energy.

At that headlong speed, it took him only a moment to reach the brush and plunge out of sight, but the noise of his hasty retreat came back as he broke his way through the barrier, not stopping for anything. Then the sounds grew fainter.

Respite at such a moment, when he had expected none, left Jim a little dazed. He had put up a good fight, but that blow over the head had left him more weakened than he had thought, not at all up to snuff. Now his reactions were a little slow. He turned his head, partly raising up, saw what Collier had seen, and felt some of the same surge of terror.

That grizzly which his horse had smelled had been more than a set of tracks. It was there now, not thirty feet away—a monstrous animal, the biggest one that he had ever seen, and he had encountered several of the big ones, both dead and alive.

This one was very much alive—standing there, head lowered, little eyes surveying him near-sightedly but watchfully, with a slightly puzzled expression. The huge head, thrust forward beyond that great ruff of muscle, gave the bear the appearance of being humpbacked.

Whether the smell of Donney's blood had attracted the bear, or if it had just happened to wander there at that moment was hard to guess.

From its attitude, Jim guessed that the latter alternative to be true. It did not act surly, he saw, merely curious, and his own fear ebbed a little. But a grizzly bear was always an unpredictable varmint, never one to trifle with.

Collier, spurred by terror and the suddenness of the thing, had acted on instinct, not stopping to think of anything else, not even the ring.

Running, though he had probably not reasoned it out, was risky. That was to court the risk of attracting the grizzly's unfavorable attention and having it come after him. That had not happened, perhaps because Jim had still been there to watch.

Nothing had happened, so far, and Collier had gotten away. Jim might be able to do the same— or he might not make two jumps before the bear would be infuriated and charge. There was no way of guessing, but a wrong guess could be fatal.

Jim saw something, a gleam of metal among the leafy mold, nearly buried by it. The reflection of the sun on one of the dropped six-shooters. It was not far off. He half slid toward it, moving slowly, keeping his eyes on the grizzly. The big silvertip was still watching with interest, but he made no hostile move. Jim's hand slid out, and his fingers closed on the gun-barrel, drew it toward him.

The feel of it in his hand was a comfortable thing. Up to a short time before, one shot at a time was the best a man could do, even in such an emergency as this. Being able to shoot six times, as fast as you could work the trigger, was like honey on bread.

Not that he intended to try it unless he had to. Even six shots from a Colt might not stop a grizzly, though they might reach fatal spots. The rush of a grizzly was like the wind—not to be stopped or turned aside, even by death. A bear could be dying, and still maul his slayer beyond recognition. Jim had seen that happen on the trail west, and he did not in the least blame Collier for being scared.

On the other hand, the feel of the gun was comforting. Jim waited, not moving, his nerves steady again. It was probably safer, the way the big fellow was acting, than to try to run.

The next minute drew out like hours. The grizzly still stood there, watching him, perhaps a little puzzled as to what he was. But nothing had stirred its anger, and the bear was not hungry. With a slow deliberateness, the big fellow turned, lumbered ponderously away and out of sight.

Jim released a lungful of stale air. As he got to his feet, he discovered an unsteadiness in his legs. He saw the other dropped gun, off a little way, and picked it up too. Now that trouble seemed to be over, he was ready for it.

His glance strayed to Hank Donney, lying where he had fallen. He had been off where the short-sighted grizzly probably had not seen him at all, which was just as well. Looking at him, Jim felt hysterical laughter bubbling in his throat, so that he had to fight it down. Donney had tried to kill him, and Collier had aimed to do the same. It had been a grizzly bear which had been his friend in the pinch.

Suddenly he remembered the ring, and where he had seen Collier put it down, on top of the boulder. It was still there. He picked it up, and saw that it was open.

The silver cayuse still reared, but differently from before. It was actually a lid now, which had lifted up as Collier worked the secret catch, to reveal a tiny opening beneath.

Collier had said something about it. It was apparent to Jim that he had known a lot more about those rings, than he was telling. Not only had the insignia of the cayuse served as a password and identification among the members of the Committee who had once owned the rings, but secret messages could be carried in them as well.

There was a tiny folded bit of paper tucked in this one. A message, beyond a doubt, and of sufficient importance so that Collier had not hesitated at murder to get hold of it.

The irony of it was that, having finally gotten the ring and opened it, he should have been distracted before he could have a look. Whatever it told was still a secret, so far as Collier was concerned.

Excitement coursed through Jim. His first impulse was to dig the paper out and see what it said. But he checked the gesture. This was no time for that. Collier, if he remembered the ring, as he would soon do, might take a notion to come back and attack from ambush. Or he might have gotten a rifle or other gun from wherever he had left his horse. The grizzly might still be close at hand, and a grizzly was always unpredictable, swift to change from one mood to a more truculent one.

He studied the ring closely, to see if he could figure out the catch, but he could not be sure of it. So it wouldn't do to shut it up again. That would protect the message inside—too well properly. But if he wore the ring, he might lose the paper on the way back.

His shirt was in rags, nearly torn off him. He pulled loose a square of whole cloth, carefully wrapped the ring in that, and placed it in his pants pocket. When he got back to camp, he'd have a look. Besides, the ring really belonged to Jeanne, and she would be as much interested in what it contained as he was.

He found his horse a quarter of a mile away, over its fright now and peacefully getting its dinner. It had no enthusiasm for returning to the spot, and still less when he wanted to load a dead man into the saddle, but he managed the job.

With his cayuse laden down, it was necessary to walk, leading the horse, and his return was slow. It was mid-afternoon when he came back to the camp, and Jeanne sprang up at sight of him and started eagerly forward, calling out, then halted at sight of what was in the saddle.

"What—what has happened, Jeem?" she asked.

"Plenty," he retorted with a reassuring grin. "But it's all worked pretty well, at that." He explained what had happened, except for the ring, which he wanted to reserve for a surprise. Jeanne's eyes were on his face as he recounted events, and there was a look in them which made his own pulse beat faster. At the conclusion, she nodded simply.

"Then it is all right," she said. "The ring has been lucky, after all. No matter what comes, you come through it alive. Eef—if anything really bad had happened to you, Jeem, I—I do not think I could stand it."

"I guess my luck is runnin' high, all right, these days," he acknowledged, and a trace of added color crept into her cheeks as she caught his glance. "Why, these days," he went on, with a warming enthusiasm and a clarity of thought which surprised himself. "I know what I want to do, and life means somethin'. Before I met you, I was plumb fiddle-footed, always lookin' for somethin', without even quite knowin' it—or havin' any notion what it was I wanted, even."

Jeanne was a child of nature, unsophisticated. But she grew suddenly shy now, as though understanding instinctively, and better than he, where these thoughts were leading him. She quickly changed the subject.

"He must be buried now, I suppose? Shall I call some of the boys to do it?"

"Where is everyone, anyway?" Jim demanded, noting the deserted look of the camp.

"They are spread out around, watching the othairs," Jeanne explained. "And Alice, she ees with Bob somewhere. They seem to like each other ver' much."

"We'll call some of them," Jim agreed. "But I didn't bring Donney back here just to bury him. I could have rolled a log aside and scooped out a place under that a lot easier. I had a hunch he'd be useful back here. Now we'll see if I'm right."

Jeanne did not ask questions. She was a competent little person, more accustomed to acting than to talking, and she had complete confidence in the ability of Jeem to do anything which he undertook. It was sometimes a little frightening, the faith which she placed in him. Jim hoped that he could live up to it now.

He found a couple of the crew, sprawled comfortably where they could keep an eye on the buildings. They looked at him in astonishment, reading the signs of the desperate struggle that he had engaged in, but they did not ask questions.

"We've seen the whole bunch of 'em, one time or another today, exceptin' Donney," they reported. "Ain't saw hide ner hair of him. They act kind of uneasy, the rest of them, like there was a skunk under the house and they was scairt to smoke it out, and twice as scairt not to."

"Go bring my horse up here, and you'll see where Donney is," Jim instructed, and raised his voice in a hail to the buildings. There was a minute of suspicious silence; then, as he repeated that he wanted to parley, someone answered.

"Go ahead and talk, if ye like—though 'twon't do no good, not till Donney gets back. He's out scoutin' around—and he'll sneak back through yore lines easy as he went out, once he gets a mind to."

That sounded like a brag to keep their own spirits up. Jim grinned, but held on to his trump card.

"That so? Might not be so easy, next time. Ain't you fellers had about enough? You ain't got half the chance of a chicken with a weasel under its wing. You're on the wrong side, of the law and everything else. Even Collier is against you, the way things are."

That shot told. Only an uneasy silence answered him. Jim went on.

"You've got two choices. If the bunch of you surrender now, and turn over Margarita and Tony in good shape, and the buildings the same way, I'll let you all go where you please. But if you make a fight of it, we'll just come ahead and kill you off like a nest of cornered mice. That won't do anybody any good, exceptin' maybe the country. You haven't a chance. You ought to know it."

Again there was an uneasy silence. Evidently they had come to pretty much the same conclusion. But they had been hired for the job, and there was a certain amount of loyalty in them.

"We can't do that," was the almost plaintive retort. "Ye'll have to talk to Donney when he gets back. If ye try a fight, we can get as many of ye as youn's can get of us."

"I doubt it," Jim retorted bluntly. "But if you want Donney to decide—he's back already. Here, take a look at him."

Boldly he walked ahead, leading his horse, with

the slumped figure of Donney still tied in the saddle. He heard a muffled exclamation, and knew that he risked a bullet, but he kept on without stopping.

"Donney's dead," he said. "You can see that. But I didn't kill him. He hid in the brush, and tried to kill me. Come close to making a go of it, too. Managed to club me down, and was aimin' to finish me when Collier shot him. Collier had been followin' me too. And I reckon you boys don't need more'n one guess as to why Collier killed him—and it sure wasn't because he wanted to save my bacon."

He stopped, waiting for that to sink in. They knew well enough what he meant. He went on evenly.

"Collier's still footlose. But I took the trouble to bring Donney back, for two reasons. So you could see for yourselves that it was useless to keep fightin', with nothin' left to fight for. And because I figgered you'd like to bury your boss, instead of havin' a bear or wolf feed off him tonight."

There was another period of silence, while they digested this. But the evidence was before their eyes, the conclusion inescapable. Suddenly the man who had acted as spokesman stood up, in full view.

"Reckon ye're right," he agreed. "If Donney's dead, we ain't got nothin' to fight for—we sure ain't doin' it for Collier now. We're surrenderin'. You call the tune."

Eighteen

The reunion between Jeanne and Margarita was rather reminiscent of an over-anxious moose reunited with her calf. Margarita gathered Jeanne into her arms as though she had been a baby, exclaiming and crooning over her.

Tony, too, was excitedly happy at the turn of events. The even tenor of life at the Ranch of the Giants had been cruelly shattered, but some of the pieces could be picked up again, and to be out from under the domination of Hank Donney made the boy almost hysterical in his relief.

Being under a roof, and in possesion again, helped a lot. Collier was still somewhere in the vicinity, and Jim did not make the mistake of underestimating him. Collier was dangerous, implacable. But they had the ring back, and Collier was alone, without a crew to back him up, even indirectly. Things could have been a lot worse.

The next morning, he would be able to set the crew at work on some of the badly needed jobs about the ranch. Those who could swing a scythe would get at the hay. Others would start to rounding up the cattle, branding the younger stock. There was plenty to do.

After a little, a good bunch of marketable beef could be driven out to the mining camps, such as Gold Town, and sold. They would find a ready market, and restore the finances of the ranch to a point where things could be handled smoothly again.

Jim was planning this in the back of his mind, even while he remembered the ring in his pocket. If, by some chance, it should yield a clue to hidden treasure, as the governor had suggested might be a possibility, that would be something else again.

It was plain enough that Collier was hoping for something like that. Nothing else would attract him, Jim was convinced. For himself, he was not particularly interested in treasure, aside from the excitement of trying to find something long hidden, not counting on it as a tangible asset. Cattle, on the other hand, was something that had a ready market value.

Hank Donney's crew had buried their former boss and departed, promising in return for freedom that they would not cause any more trouble. Washed up, in a fresh shirt, and having disposed of a good supper, which Margarita had prepared in celebration of the turn of events, he felt better.

Reese and Alice had gone for a stroll by moonlight. That suited Jim. He liked Bob Reese, and he liked the red-head. This looked like a chance for her to make a fresh start in life. With them out of the way, there was no need to say anything to them about the secret of the ring. That, after all, chiefly concerned Jeanne.

He turned to her now, explaining that the silver cayuse had been Collier's real interest, and how he had gotten the ring open, but had not had time to get the real secret out of it. He saw her eyes glow with interest.

"I thought we could have a look now," he suggested. "Though, come to think of it, there's a right nice moon. Mebby Bob and Alice have the right idea. Would you rather take a stroll by moonlight, too?"

"I would rather see the ring," Jeanne said promptly. "The moon, it shines 'most every night. Are you not burning weeth curiosity, Jeem?"

"Well, I am a bit curious," he confessed. "But haven't you ever taken a walk by moonlight—with somebody?"

"Never," Jeanne denied, and colored as she met his glance. "The moon, eet is foolish! Now about the ring!"

He pulled the cloth out of his pocket, unwrapped the ring, and handed it to her.

"The way that paper's tucked in there, it'll have to be pried out with a pin or somethin', looks like," he said, and cautioned her against over-eagerness. "Better be pretty careful. It may be about ready to crumple up and go all to pieces."

"I will be mos' careful," she promised, and was true to her word. Unfolded and spread out, it was still just a tiny bit of paper—a square not much more than an inch in size, but fortunately of a good quality of paper. Seemingly no one had counted on the possibility of it remaining hidden in the ring for more than a few days, or weeks at most. But it still seemed to be in good condition, with no tendency to crumple.

Jeanne spread it out on the table before them, glanced at it, puzzled, then turned it over. Her voice was sharp with disappointment.

"But eet is blank, Jeem," she protested. "There is no writing on it—nothing!"

Jim had seen that for himself. His head was close to Jeanne's dark one, and a faintly disturbing perfume seemed to emanate from her hair, which made it difficult for him to keep his full attention on the matter in hand.

He had felt the same sharp shock of disappointment. Then he had discounted it. After all, no one would be apt to take the trouble to hide a piece of blank paper in the ring. The game they played had been far too grim for any foolishness among the wearers of the silver cayuse. He picked the little square up carefully and held it to the light.

As he had guessed, it had been written on carefully in ink, but that had been a good many years before, and the ink had been of doubtful quality. It had faded, so that the paper appeared to be blank. But, held to the light, the writing still showed, faintly, but legible enough to real. There were just five words:

"*Rancho el Gianto*. The Giants."

Jeanne too, was deciphering them, murmuring the words aloud. She looked at him in bewilderment.

"The Giants?" she repeated. "Those are the great tall rocks—but what does it mean? I have ridden there many times, Jeem. There ees nothing there— or I at least have never seen it."

"You've never been lookin' for any hidden treasure," Jim pointed out. "If there is any there, it's been well hid, of course. And I have a hunch that this is just about what this means," he went on in mounting excitement. "Collier wanted to get hold of the ranch, so he must have had some reason to think there was somethin' like this somewhere on the ranch. He didn't just want land."

Jeanne was catching some of his enthusiasm.

"We weel have a look and see, 'eh?" she said. "Maybe we find something."

"Maybe," Jim agreed. "We'll sure do our best. And if we do find it, it will belong to you, Jeanne. This was your father's ring, that held the secret. And the Ranch of the Giants belongs to you now. So, on any count, it should belong to you."

"If we find it, eet will be as much yours as mine, Jeem," she assured him simply. "Without you, what would I have? Or be able to do? Nothing."

He did not argue the question. They had yet to find it, and it might not amount to much. His mind went to another angle of the case. If there was hidden treasure, regardless of the part in collecting it that the wearers of the silver cayuse might have had, it had probably been stolen, originally, from wealthy landowners, all up and down the length of California. Perhaps even from far parts of the earth.

Those original owners would be the legal ones now—save for the fact that it would probably be impossible, at this late date, ever to restore anything to the rightful owners. If there was hidden treasure, and they found it, it would have to be in jewels and gold, such imperishable things. All other loot, rich silks and what not, which might have had great value at the time, would long since have rotted in any ordinary storage place.

Diamonds, rubies, pearls, gold—whether in bars or coins—were things which, freed of their original settings, would be impossible to identify, especially after such a lapse of time. Even more to the point, and even if anything could be identified and the name and address of the owner ascertained, how could such an owner, or even his heirs, be found now? A revolution had taken place in California in the years since the treasure had been hidden.

And with it, as he could see everywhere he went, tragedy had struck. California had been a quiet, pastoral land, a gay and delightful place, by all accounts—at least for the big land owners who had possessed it. It had been a land of moonlight and roses.

But that was part of the past. They had been dispossessed or killed—like the Gonzales. And that was the pattern, not the exception, clear across the state. True, here and there a former grandee, with his title perhaps dating straight back to an ancient grant from the King of Spain, still managed to hold on to what was his. But they were the exceptions, not the rule.

There was plenty of scum from the four corners of the earth there in the land, attracted by the promise of easy money. Men like Collier and Donney, who had no respect at all for the rights of others. There were plenty of others who were honest men and women, who had no intention of usurping the rights of others, but who had contrived to do so in one way or another nonetheless.

The case of John Sutter was a good example. Sutter owned the land where gold had originally been found. He was a pioneer, a man who had warmly welcomed the change from Mexican rule to that of the United States. A rich man, and a natural leader. He had been a leading contender for the governorship of the new state.

Yet he was now being crowded off his own land by the newcomers, who simply in and filed on claims and squatted there, not in tens but in hundreds or thousands.

Part of the cause was thoughtlessness, part selfishness. To the average newcomer, anyone of another race was a foreigner, and not quite so good or worthy of ownership as himself. It was mankind's ancient curse again in action. A Spaniard or a Mexican was at a disadvantage to start with.

It was not right or just, and certainly, from what Jim himself had seen, citizens like the Gonzales were vastly better and preferable to newcomers like the Donneys or the Colliers. But none of that altered the facts of the case.

So, with the old owners scattered, dispossessed,

vanished, there would be little chance of restoring any ancient treasure to them. And Jeanne at least had excellent claims to it.

The girl had been deep in thought. She turned to him now, her eyes glowing.

"Oh, Jeem, isn't it exciting?" she demanded. "This will be so much fun—I never thought that there was anything like that to my ring!"

She took it up again, studying it with keen eyes, and after a minute she exclaimed:

"See, here ees the catch! And so cleverly hidden! It is one of the hoofs of the cayuse—and if you press on it—but if you press with a finger, eet is too big, and does no good. Just something like a pin, to move the one tiny point—"

She showed him, so that he could see the catch, on some spring-like arrangement. The silversmith who had made these rings originally had been a superb craftsman. She closed the ring again, opened it, gleefully triumphant at having mastered its secret.

"But I want you to keep it, Jeem," she said, serious again. "I think eet will still be good luck." She slipped it back on his finger. "And now, I think, since we both know what it says, we had better destroy this, yes?" she asked, holding up the tiny square of paper.

Jim agreed, and they watched it burn. The next day, after the others were at work, they would go to the Giants and see what they could find. It was not apt to be easy, finding something which had lain hidden all these years. But they would at least make a thorough search.

Then he frowned as he considered the plan. It would be safer not to go, just the two of them. He'd better take at least one of the crew as well. For Collier would instantly guess what they were doing, reasoning correctly that the ring had pointed to the treasure being hidden thereabouts.

And Collier would be watching their every movement from then on. He probably would not interfere with them as long as they were searching. But if they happened to be lucky, and to find it— that would be a different story.

In that case, he was the sort who would go to any lengths to get it.

If they failer to find it, they would still have shown the spot to Collier, and he would of course have a try himself. And he might well know things, secrets from the past, which would help him. So if they failed to find it, it would be a good idea to keep the place under observation at all times, just to see what luck Collier might have.

Jim had been aiming to have Reese act as foreman while he himself was busy with this job. Now, on second thought, he decided to set the rest of the crew to work, and to take Reese and Alice along on the treasure hunt.

They could be trusted, and all of them together would be none too many for the job, if they wanted to do it right—and to guard against Collier.

Nineteen

The Giants rose up starkly as they approached them, two huge monoliths of stone set close against the rising hill behind, as if they were the portals to a gateway, or perhaps sentries placed on guard. The fancy pleased Jim. Maybe they were sentries, guarding the treasure.

There would be no profit, he knew, in a hit or miss search. Whoever had hidden treasure in the first place had been at pains to see to it that it should remain hidden from all prying eyes. The fact that people had been coming past there during all the intervening years, without even suspecting that anything of import was concealed, was proof enough that the original hiders had done a good job.

"We'll mark the place off in sections, then explore a section at a time," he explained. "We'll begin with the most likely spots first—around the Giants themselves. But it won't be easy."

He studied the landscape speculatively, trying to imagine that he had come there with something worth hiding, seeking to pick out a likely place. There were any number that would do well enough —small holes back in the base of the cliff, or in the big giants themselves—holes averaging a foot or so in size and usually of about the same depth. Something might have been cached back in one of these, the hole filled over to conceal it.

Here was one slab of rock, ten feet wide and all of thirty feet high, which had cracked loose at some time in the past from the upper side of the left-hand giant, and had slid to the ground. It rested now, half against its parent, half against the side of the bluff behind.

"Earthquake," Jim guessed. "It would take quite a shock, too, to jar a chunk like that down, even if it was a little loose."

"Glad I wasn't here when it happened." Reese grinned. "These big boys look solid enough now, though, if anything should start jiggin' again."

Jim had no fear of anything like that. But he did have the feeling, as they worked, that Collier was watching them, and that was not so pleasant.

It was, as he had expected, a slow, unexciting job. Covering one marked off section at a time, poking into those holes in the rock, tapping for something loose, going over the ground, foot by foot. By noon, they had covered two thirds of the likely territory, and had found nothing which even remotely resembled a clue.

"The trouble is," Reese grumbled, "they might have dug a hole, y'see, anywhere—'n after all these years, there ain't a blame thing t' tell where it could've been. That's the mischief of't—nothin' to go by."

"It wouldn't be any fun, hunting for something that was easy to find," Jeanne said practically. "And you'd know that it wasn't worth much, if that was the way they had hid it to start with."

By evening, however, when they had gone over every likely bit of ground as carefully as they knew how, they were a bit discouraged.

"We'll try again tomorrow," Jim announced. "Maybe we'll get some new ideas by then."

"How about keepin' watch?" Reese asked. "Still aimin' to do that?"

"I'll stay hereabouts tonight," Jim said. "The

rest of you go on back. I'll make out to go with you, then shadder my way back to where I can keep an eye out."

The night passed quietly enough. If Collier was anywhere around, he made no open move. Apparently he was going on the theory that they might as well do their best first. If they failed, he might try his hand.

By noon of the next day, Jim was ready to confess himself stumped. Those two words, "The Giants," probably referred to the big rocks, but they might be wrong in supposing that they indicated a hiding place for treasure. They might have meant something else entirely. Sobered, they withdrew a little way to eat dinner, and were in the middle of the meal, all thoughtfully silent, when Jeanne lifted an arm and pointed.

Following her gesture, they saw it—a grizzly bear, leisurely approaching them. Whether this was the big fellow that had frightened Collier away the other day or not, he was certainly big enough. So far, the bear had not scented them, and came on, unconscious of danger. And then, even as they saw him, he stopped, swinging his big head from side to side, growling and testing the air.

The fellow was plainly in a truculent mood, not disposed to turn aside or go tamely about other business. Reese made as if to rise, then stopped at Jim's gesture.

They waited a moment, until it was certain that the grizzly had located them. He stood there, his mood still uncertain, growling, and the low mutter of it was taking on angry overtones, changing to a savage snarl. Again Reese's eyes met Jim's, and this time he nodded.

Since his previous encounter, Jim had taken the precaution not to be caught only with a revolver. A six-gun was excellent in its way, since it could shoot six times instead of one, but a forty-five bullet, unless it was lucky enough to reach exactly the right spot, could be more like a pea-shooter against an angry half-ton or so of bear. And this fellow would come close to that in weight.

A rifle would shoot only once, but the heavy ball was a lot more effective. Jim and Reese both had rifles, standing loaded and ready, leaning against a tree a few feet away.

They reached them; the girls were also on their feet and backing away. The grizzly, nearsighted as it was, had not been too sure of them before, but now that they had moved it had seem them. They waited, leaving it up to the big silvertip to decide. If he changed his mind and go away, that would suit them fine. As Reese had remarked only that morning, when standing his rifle against the tree, he hadn't lost any grizzlies.

But today the bear had no intention of turning or leaving them in possession. Jim knew the signs. He was getting ready to come ahead, and when he came, it would be with a rush.

"You take him," Jim ordered. "I'll hold my fire, in case you don't stop him."

Reese nodded, not speaking. He was steady as a rock, but Jim could see the tiny beads of sweat which had popped on his forehead, and he knew just how he felt. The girls were going farther back, but to face a grizzly at twenty paces was hard on any man's nerves. Anything might happen. Even if both of them hit where they aimed with those heavy slugs, that might not stop him in time.

Reese's big gun thundered, shattering the silence, but the grizzly, his fury worked up to a fighting pitch, had unloosed a sudden roar which dwarfed the noise of the rifle and plunged ahead, a moment before Reese pulled trigger. Just an instant, but that been enough to throw the aim off, and the shot, so nearly as Jim could tell, was a miss. And now the grizzly was rolling down at them like a juggernaut of doom.

Jim fired in turn. Shooting at a charging bear was not so easy as aiming at a motionless target, but at such a range he could hardly miss. Then he was jerking at his revolver, since there was no time to reload, pumping more lead at the still onrushing grizzly.

It looked as though nothing could check that rush now. But Reese, still cool enough, had begun using his short-gun, and under the rain of lead, the rush slackened, and finally the grizzly rolled over, sliding forward another two or three feet before it was still.

"Whew!" Reese mopped at his face. "That's the first grizzly I've ever tackled, and so far as I'm concerned, I'll not be mad if'n it's the last."

Jim said nothing. He was busily reloading his rifle for possible emergencies, and seeing him, Reese followed his example. Not until then did they approach the bear, which by that time was dead enough.

Convinced of that, and now that the danger was

past, Reese examined it with fresh interest, his pride growing. Then he looked up.

"Here's three-four holes where we used our revolvers," he said. "And one big one from a rifle bullet, right through the heart. That's what stopped him, all right. But I can't find but one rifle wound. One must've missed him."

It was Alice who answered that.

"You missed him, Bob," she said. "I could tell."

"Did I?" Reese shook his head ruefully. "I sure didn't aim to—but he made a right spry start."

Since it was evident that one of them had missed, and Alice declared that he had, Reese accepted it without argument, but Jim could see that he was still not convinced that it was his shot which had gone wild. Just for his own satisfaction, Jim decided to try to make sure.

The bluff, and one of the Giants, had been right in line with Reese's shot, some distance behind the bear. Jim crossed to the spot, looked around for a minute, and saw where the bullet had gone. It had hit an edge of the big slab of rock which had slid off from the giant at some time in the past, and the hole, shoulder high, just the size of a bullet, was so fresh that it could not be mistaken.

Looking at it, Jim felt a sudden surge of excitement. Near its edge, the slab was not very thick—only two or three inches, apparently, though he had supposed it to be thicker. Not only had the bullet gone clear through it, but a crack or so radiated from the hole toward the edge of the slab. And behind and beyond the hole was blackness.

Jeanne came running up, seeing that he had found something, and the others followed. Reese, seeing this unmistakable proof of where his bullet had gone, shook his head ruefully.

"Guess I was wilder'n I figgered," he confessed. "I knew I was scared—but not that bad."

"You were holdin' just about on him, if he hadn't rushed just as he did," Jim assured him. "But maybe that was a lucky miss." Excitement had crept into his voice, as he took his knife and commenced to pry at the cracked rock.

"Lucky? How do you m—"

Reese's voice trailed off as a chunk of the rock came loose—a trianguler-shaped slab, several inches wide. Behind it was what Jim had noticed before —darkness. And darkness was not to be expected, for the slab had seemed to rest solidly against the side of the bluff.

Yet here was empty space instead of the solid hill, and Jim knew what that must mean. He broke off another, larger chunk of the rock, and now there was no mistaking it. There was an opening in the hill—the mouth of a cave. An indistinct sound, like the sighing of wind in the tree tops, could be heard now.

"A cave!" Reese breathed. "Well, what do you know about that! Do y'think—" He stared at the slab, and shook his head.

"Nope, that wouldn't be it," he decided. "No chance of them hidin' that stuff back in a cave here. How'd they know about it, any more'n we would? And even if they did, that slab'll weigh ten tons. No chance of shovin' it out of the way, then settin' it back for a door; after they got through."

"But you might be right, at that," Jim insisted, conviction growing in him. "Like I said yesterday, that chunk of rock must've been shook down, one time or another, by nothin' less than an earthquake. What if it tumbled down *after* they'd hid the loot back in this cave? The thing happened a good many years ago, remember."

The others were beginning to catch his excitement now. Jeanne's eyes were shining.

"Now I remember, Jeem," she exclaimed. "Pedro, he was here on the ranch for many years. Once I heard him say that he had seen a cave, here by the Giants. He sounded puzzled, as though he could not understand why he had' seen it once, then could not find it again."

"That's the answer, all right," Jim said jubilantly. "He'd sort of forgot just where it was, likely, and after the slab had slid and covered it, he wasn't quite sure. But it's proof that the cave used to be open."

None of them voiced the hope surging in them now. If the cave had been here, then had been blocked in such a manner for years, it would have been an even more effective hiding place than could have been counted on. And whatever had been inside when the slab fell must still be there.

Most of the slab was thick, except near the edge. Jim hammered off another chunk, tossed it aside, and stopped at Jeanne's sudden exclamation.

She was pointing now to something scratched crudely on the side of the rocky wall of the cave, just revealed as this other stone was gotten out of the way. A rearing horse—the sign of the silver cayuse.

Twenty

There was no doubt in their minds now that they were on the right track at last. The rearing cayuse had been scratched there to mark the spot, of course, and it would mean nothing to any casual observer, though furnishing a definite clue to the initiate. And because nature had taken a hand, sending a quake to shake loose that big slab from the side of the giant, the secret had remained doubly hidden all these years.

The grizzly was forgotten now. They cleared away more of the rock, until there was an opening big enough to walk through. With the light shining in, it was possible to see something of the cave itself now, and one look showed that it was no ordinary cave, but something approaching the proportions of a cavern.

The original opening had apparently not been much bigger than what they had cleared out now —a passageway some five feet high about three in width. It led back, tunnel-like, for about three or four feet, through solid rock, before widening to the proportions of a big room.

This room was at least twenty feet high, and the air in it was rather stale, though it was rapidly freshening now that the opening had been cleared out. Probably brush had helped to conceal the doorway in the old days, so that only someone who had explored closely would have guessed at the presence of a cave. All of those remembered factors would have made it an excellent choice for a hiding place for the bandits' loot.

The room was all of thirty feet wide, the walls of solid rock. Just how far back it led was a little hard to judge, since the light did not shine far enough to show it. But, back fifteen or twenty feet, something did show, dark and forbidding— running water.

Here, Jim could see, was an underground stream, swirling out of an opening at the one side, running untrammeled the width of the cavern, then being sucked under again with a gurgle of protest. It was that sound they had heard at first, like far-off wind.

The stream looked deep, bottomless in the darkness, and quite wide. They eyed it, a little awed, and Jim tossed a small piece of stone experimentally. It seemed to hit on a rocky wall at the opposite side, then plopped straight down into the water again.

"Nice place, ain't it?" Reese muttered, and his voice sounded a little awed. "All the comforts of home—a roof over yore head, runnin' water—but I don't like it."

That pretty well summed up what the others felt, but it was a promising place for their purpose. They went back outside and found a couple of chunks of pitch pine, and with these for torches, resumed their inspection.

The light reflected back eerily from the far side of the stream now, showing only a smooth, upright wall on the far side. The water ran deep and cold to the extreme edge. The rocky floor of the cavern had been washed by the stream in years long past to a polished smoothness. It showed the faint, ancient-looking scratches of hob-nailed shoes, but that was all. Or those might have been made by some tool, Jim decided.

The pertinent and chilling fact about it was that everything back in here—floor, walls and all—was of solid, smooth rock, with no break or hole where anything might have been hidden.

Above their heads, however, was a projecting ledge of rock, a sort of shelf, and sight of it aroused their hopes again. A chest or sack might well have been set back up on there. Reese boosted him, and Jim climbed onto it, with one of the torches for light. It was necessary to go carefully, for a slip would send him off and into the stream below, since the edge of the shelf was right above the edge of the water.

He saw Jeanne's face, a little pale in the torch-glow, as she watched him in silence, expectant, hopeful. But up there there was nothing but emptiness.

He scrambled down again, and at sight of his face, the hope drained out of Jeanne's. She had been counting so much on this, he knew—and there was nothing there. And nowhere else to look.

Probably there had been something there once. The message in the ring, the rearing cayuse scratched outside, seemed to indicate as much. But if loot had been hidden there, then it must be that someone had come and gotten it again, before the slab of rock had slid to block the opening. So, despite their hopes, and Collier's, it had apparently been gone—perhaps divided up and spent—these many years.

It was disappointing, particularly since there was no other place left to search, no hope of finding it now. For himself, Jim did not care, but he had wanted Jeanne to be pleased. But she was already rallying, smiling a little to hide her disappointment.

"What good would it do, anyhow?" she asked practically. "We have enough already—and much work to do on the ranch. Now we can forget this foolishness and get at it."

Alice crossed to her and put an arm across her shoulders.

"You've sure got the right idea," she agreed. "And plenty of spunk. Well, it was fun while it lasted."

They went back out into the open air. The suck and gurgle of the dark waters echoed unpleasantly behind them. It was good, fresh water, very cold, as Jim had found, but it was deep and dark and somehow on a par with the dark and bloody deeds that had been associated with that vanished treasure.

Men had schemed and fought and died to possess it, and for most of them, too, it had been an empty dream.

"Do we keep watch here any longer?" Reese asked practically. "It'll be my turn, tonight, if we do. Though if Collier wants to snoop around—he'll be a lot sma'ter'n what I figger, to find anything."

Jim felt the same way about it. It was possible that Collier, from his old knowledge and associations, might have some sort of a clue which they lacked. But how it could do him any good, Jim couldn't see. The trail had been plain enough, up to there. The message in the ring, the rearing cayuse scratched above the cave door. Collier had been right in his hunch that the loot had been brought there and hidden.

But that had been long ago, and something had happened to it in the years between. There was no place in the cave where it could be. If Collier wanted to have a look, that was all right. But as Jeanne said, there was work to be done, and that was of first importance.

"We won't bother here any more," Jim said decisively. "Let's skin that grizzly. It'll make a nice rug. Then we'll go home, and tomorrow we'll start the round-up, while the boys who can swing a scythe go on with the haying."

Jeanne was in full accord with him on this. After all, the ranch was her pride, her whole life almost. It had to be taken care of. That was what the Gonzales would have wanted.

Jim allowed his mind to dwell briefly on the old man. Had he, by any chance, been involved in that affair of nearly a score of years before? Had he known anything about the treasure, possibly opening the ring, finding the secret, and going and getting the loot? That was a possibility, but it seemed far-fetched and remote now. The thing to do was to forget all about hidden treasure.

Considerable hay had already been cut. There were some good men at that work, and one of them, leaning on his scythe to mop the sweat from his face, confessed that it was good to have such a job again.

"Me, I been a farmer all my life," he said proudly, albeit a little wistfully. "I'm crowdin' fifty now, and ought to be old enough to have a smatterin' of sense. Guess I didn't have—leavin' a good farm, chasin' clear acrost the country for gold that I never saw ary sign of."

He shook his head, then looked proudly at the new-mown, fragrant hay.

"But I used to be able to beat any man I ever knew swingin' the scythe, and I ain't forgot how. Makes me feel more respectable, like, to be doin' real work again."

With a crew like that, men who had chased their dream to rainbow's end and been disillusioned, the work would be done, *El Gianto* built up again to its former cmmanding position as a great ranch.

The next few hours were busy ones. Cattle were something which Jim knew pretty well. He had driven oxen as a boy, milked cows. On the road west he had learned to shoe them, to ride a cayuse and swing a rope. And now he had a trained cow pony between his legs, one which knew enough to make up for any deficiencies in knowledge which he might have. A man had to be a good rider and strictly on his toes to ride such a horse when following a dogie through the brush, or cutting out a calf. Otherwise it would turn when a cow did, with such amazing speed that it would be easy to keep right on over its head.

But with a horse that knew its business, it was easy to handle cattle, if you could stay in the saddle and dab a loop over a pair of horns at the right moment. This, too, was hard work—branding, hazing the gathering herd gradually in the way that they were supposed to go, and all the rest. But like swinging a scythe, it was satisfying work.

The girls were riding with them, each doing the job as well as any man could. Alice had demonstrated that she was as much at home in the saddle as on the ground, despite the trick which she had played on him at first. Reese, who was a better than average horseman himself, was loud in his praises of her skill. But Reese, Jim guessed, would be pretty well pleased with anything that the red-head did now.

Jeanne, raised on the big ranch, was every bit as good as Alice, and she had the advantage of knowing the country as well. By mid-afternoon, a bunch had been rounded up from one section, and Jim saw it started back toward the buildings,

He had gotten off away from the others in his search for a stray or so, and now he saw that he was not far from the Giants. The temptation was strong. There was nothing much to do for the rest of the day, except to kept pushing that bunch along, and the others could do that nicely. He'd have a look, and see if Collier had been prowling since they left.

There was no sign of Collier's horse, but it might be hidden somewhere. Leaving his own horse, Jim proceeded on foot, going cautiously. But there was still no sign of Collier. Maybe he had seen their failure to get anywhere, had taken a look, and had come to the same conclusion as they —that there was no treasure left to be found.

The cave itself itself was just ahead. And there he saw sign, at last. Someone had been there, and had dug around in a few spots to make sure that he had not overlooked any possibilities. That would be Collier, of course. But apparently he had had no better luck than the rest of them, and must have pulled out in disgust.

Jim stepped through the opening into the cavern. The rush and gurgle of the water was as strong as ever, and he stood looking down at it, fascinated and repelled at the same time. A man down in there wouldn't stand much of a chance. If he were sucked under, into the blackness beyond, there would be no way of ever coming up again. And the water was so cold that it would soon chill even a strong swimmer.

He wondered how deep the water was. Even with a torchlight, it was impossible to see far down. It might be very deep, or perhaps only a few feet. Then he shrugged away the thought that had been in his mind. No one would think of lowering even an iron chest into the water for a hiding place. There were too many things wrong with such a cache.

Still, it was an idea. And such things as diamonds, gold, rubies, pears—water probably wouldn't hurt them. And whoever had done it in the first place would have figured on leaving them hidden in such a fashion for only a very short time, of course.

"Thinking of jumping in to have a look, Tobey?"

The voice, coming from behind him, seemed to freeze Jim for a moment. It was mocking, sardonic, edged with icy hate. He turned slowly, to see Collier standing there, a leveled revolver in his hand.

"I was in the dark, over there at the side," Collier explained with a slight gesture of his head. "I saw you coming, and so I waited. I'd been about ready to quit, same you did yesterday, and pull out. But this makes it better—a lot better."

Jim made no reply, merely watched tensely. He knew, beyond any possibility of doubt, that Collier intended to kill him. This was a perfect place for it—his body could be tossed into the water, sucked down and out of sight.

"I was pretty disappointed," Collier went on evenly. "I've hoped to get my hands on things again for a good many years now. You see, I know what was hidden here, and what it was worth. And a good bit of it belonged to me in the first place!"

His nostrils flared for a moment; then he was calm again.

"It's not pleasant, to come this close to something, after all the tribulations I've endured, and then find nothing—nothing at all. Rather a bitter pill to swallow. Like the other day, with the ring, when that grizzly interfered and you got it back."

He shook his head a little, though the gun was unwavering.

"A grizzly mauled me—once. A highly unpleasant experience. I confess to an unreasoning terror of them ever since—otherwise I'd never have run. However, it has worked out well enough—except that neither of us has had any luck. But your being here helps. A bit of sweetening at the last, as you might put it. You've gotten in my way at every turn, bothered me far too much—and that's something that I don't stand for. This time I'm going to kill you."

Jim was calculating his chances. There was only one—and that was a long one. Not the sort that he would choose under any other circumstances. But now, when there was no choice, it was that or die.

Collier had spoken his piece; his face was cold, bleak. His finger was starting to squeeze the trigger. Jim heard the crashing thunder of the gun, doubly loud in the narrow confines of the cavern, even as he flung himself back, down into those black waters.

Twenty-One

The water was like a black, icy sack being pulled shut around him, despite the fact that he had been prepared for the shock of it. He went under and down, and knew that Collier's questing bullet had missed him. The suck of the current, while not particularly strong there, was terrifying in its feel of latent power. It was fear, more than the current itself, which he knew that he had to fight against.

He straightened in the water, and his feet touched bottom for a moment. His hand, reaching up, came out in the air at the same time, so he knew now how deep it was. But now the most desperate part of the game remained to be played.

The water was no refuge—not for long. He had to get out again, or perish. Yet to get outside was to present a target for Collier's gun, with the result as inevitable as the flow of the stream.

Jim popped to the surface, playing the old, boyish trick of splashing water with his hands as he came. He heard the muffled report of the gun a second time, but Collier had been a bit over-anxious with that shot, and the lead made a chugging plop in the water beyond him. Before he could fire again, he was half drenched, with water in his face and eyes.

This was an advantage which had to be followed up fast. At the edge of the creek, Jim reached, lunging; his fingers closed on Collier's boot, at the ankle, and jerked. Frantically, Collier tried to jerk back, to kick himself free. He went down on his back, still on shore, and managed, writhing and twisting, to hold his position, still kicking, boot and spur together a nasty thing. But he had dropped his gun in the tumble.

That was all right, if he wanted it that way. Jim pulled himself out, still holding to that thrashing leg, grabbing the other one as it was aimed at his face, holding them, twisting the man down. Now that he was out of the water, the exertion was a warming thing and pleasant. The gun had slid along the slippery wet surface of the rocky floor, had reached the brink and gone in like a frog.

Collier was frantic, in the grip of a terror engendered by the Stygian stream. He had been sure of himself, of his triumph, this time, yet again he had failed, and now it had reverted again to what was becoming like a recurring nightmare—this endless struggle between Jim Tobey and himself for supremacy. This time it could not end in a draw, nor indecisively. This time it was to a finish.

Jim had crept up him, holding him helpless, wet arms engulfing him. A cold and clammy thing like the dark stream itself. Collier's terror of that was far greater than his fear of the man he fought. Here was the Styx, but no Charon with a ferry. Collier tried desperately, and fear lent him a madman's strength. He heaved himself to his feet, taking Jim along with him, flung him off and at the black pool again.

This was triumph—and then Jim Tobey's clutching fingers, dragging down along his sleeve, closed there with a grip which would not break. The very force of his effort threw Collier off-balance. Jim went out and backward hitting the water again, but Collier was with him.

They went down, locked together, into those nightmarish depths, and now the fear in Collier made him twice as dangerous. In a moment, they broke to the surface again, and Collier was no longer trying to get loose. His purpose now was to keep Jim under until the water did his work for him.

Jim reached, and Collier, remembering that throat-grip, jerked his head back frantically, and they broke apart. Again Collier lunged at him, and Jim thrashed back and down. Deep in the water, off-balance, fighting the pull of the current now, his wrist hit something sharp and hard and blunt. As he came to the surface again and brought his hand up, it had a brownish stain on it, like blood.

But for the moment he had no time to think about that. Collier seemed now to have lost his fear of the water, in his mad obsession to destroy his enemy. He thrashed forward again, swimming like a beaver, and there was no chance to evade him.

It was ludicrous, in a way. Half swimming, fighting the pull of the dark current, trying to wrestle, to duck each other under—it was like the ponderous boxing of polar bears. The really deadly thing about it was the chill of the water. Even their heavy exertions could not long keep them warm in that icy grip. It seemed as though the stream itself were fluid ice.

Again they went under, locked together. Now they were both off their feet, being dragged along, and again the nightmarish quality of the cavern ahead drove all other thoughts from Jim's mind. All that he wanted to do was to get loose, to fight his way back to the light, to the surface—to a breath of air, back to the rocky shore and the blessed comfort of lying there at ease.

It was hard to think at all now, for his thoughts seemed weighted, sluggish, like his arms, his slow-moving legs. A numbness was on them, on him—and his lungs seemed close to breaking.

Collier still clung to him, like a floating, dragging anchor. Terror gripped Jim afresh as sudden understanding came to him. Collier was dead—or close to it. But down in those black depths, with the quickening pull of the current seeking to sweep them on under the rocky overhang, his hands had set in a last frenzied, unbreaking grip as he lost consciousness—as if, in death, his resolve to take his enemy with him remained stronger than fear of death itself.

He was an incubus, like the old man of the sea,

going down, dragging Jim along with him. Terror was uppermost in Jim's mind, and unsuspected energy exploded in him. He tore loose from those clutching fingers, and his head reached the surface, so that he could suck in a deep draught of air—the sweetest thing that he had ever known.

There was life in it. But the terror was with him still, made more real by the darkness. There was daylight, but it was off at the side, and above him—a long way off upstream. For he was out of the cavern itself now, swept downstream during those terrible moments of struggle, so that he had come up under the solid wall of rock.

Here there was barely a foot of air space above his head and the solid ceiling of rock. And not far on down, where the dark took on a quality of blackness which was thick and solid and heavy, he could hear the suck and gurgle of the water as this last bit of air and life was filled up and shut away.

Too, the current was quickening. He swam, feeling the dragging weight of his own legs, the biting cold which was creeping clear through him now. He reached as far as the edge of the cavern again, not quite knowing how he did it. And there the last strength that had been in him seemed to drain out, to be flowing away downstream as surely and as swiftly as the black water ran. Try as he would, he could not advance against the current. His greatest efforts barely served to hold him in one place.

The thought came to him that he might put his feet down, and walk. But the water was over his head and the distance was too great, even if he had not been on the verge of exhaustion. He had made a good fight, but this was to be the end—with a scant twenty feet to go! Twenty feet, which might as well have been that many miles.

"Jeem! Catch the rope! Quick!"

The words came to his ears, and then he saw her, standing there on the edge of the stream—Jeanne! For a moment it seemed to him that this was a continuing part of the nightmare which gripped him. It could be nothing else. Or maybe he was dead already, and this was heaven, and she was an angel there, beckoning to him. He wanted to come to her, but he could not.

Then something touched his hand roughly, and his head cleared a little. The rope! It was a lariat rope which she had flung to him, while she held fast to the other end. He grabbed it, and tried to swim to help a little, but he could not. It took all the strength he had, all the will power, to hold fast to the rope.

But that was enough. Jeanne was pulling on it, steadily, hand over hand, drawing him through the water, closer to her. She reached down then and got a hold on him, and he could not see the desperation in her face, nor know how close she was to losing her footing on that slippery, sloping shelf, before she had him out.

For a few moments he lay there, the strength all washed out of him. But he heard her speaking to him, urgently, and that was a summons which he could not disregard. While his muscles were still lax, and his mind seemed far away from the hulk of his limp body, it was all suddenly very clear to him—the reason he had followed the long trail West, the thing that, all unwittingly, he had been searching for, the reason for living. Jeanne.

That was it. Jeanne. She was better than gold, or hidden treasure, or anything else which earth might hold. The goal that he had never quite understood, nor known about. But Jeanne was calling him, and he flopped over on his back and sat up, and managed a rather white-faced grin at her. He saw the sudden relief, the look of radiance which came to her face as he did so.

"I'm—all right," he said reassuringly. "Just a little—unsteady."

He tried to get to his feet, stumbled and would have fallen had she not caught him. It was uncanny how weak he had become. But strength was coming back, and she helped him out into the sunlight. The warmth of it, the untrammeled, free feel of space all about, was something that he had hardly dared hope to feel again.

Strength flowed back into him, out in the sun. It was the life-giver. And Jeanne's hair was like the sun. He looked at her in lazy contentment.

"How did you happen to get here—just in the nick of time?" he asked.

"I heard the gun," she explained. "So I rode—fast. I saw your horse, and I ran to the cave. At first, because it was so dark, I could see nothing—it seemed to be all empty. And I was afraid. Then I saw your face—oh, Jeem!"

She stared at space, biting her lip, her breast heaving. Jim made his voice matter of fact.

"So you threw me the rope! And I sure needed it!"

She looked at him a moment, and asked no questions. She knew with whom he had been fighting, of course, and Collier was not there. Something like a sob caught and strangled in her throat as she looked quickly away again.

"Oh, Jeem," she said. "I was praying—"

The words faltered, and she walked away, came back presently. It seemed to him that she had suddenly become a woman. Her words now were casual enough.

"Do you think that you can ride now?" she asked.

Jim nodded, stood up, and stared curiously at his wrist. It was not cut, after all, not bloodstained —but there was still a trace of brown stain on his arm.

"Sure I can ride," he agreed. "But not just yet. There's one thing I want to do first. I'm not sure, Jeanne, so don't get your hopes up too high—but I think maybe I've found that treasure."

"Found it?" she echoed, girlishly eager again. "Oh, Jeem! Where?"

"See this?" He showed her his wrist, grinning quizzically. "Know what it is?"

She frowned at it, not quite understanding.

"Eet—it looks like—like rust," she suggested a little doubtfully.

"And that's just what it is," Jim agreed. "Down in the water there, I hit something hard and sharp with my arm—and this rubbed off on it. It's rust, all right. That must have been the edge of an iron chest—what else could it be?"

Her eyes were alight now with the old eagerness; then she shook her head.

"Eef it is—then what of it?" she asked. "I do not want you to go down in that water again—not for anything, ever. I—oh, Jeem, it hurt me, here in my heart, when I thought that the water had you. It is so dark!"

"Sure you don't want me to go, even for lost treasure?" he teased.

She shook her head.

"No! Not even for that. Eet is not worth it—not now, anyway. You are tired, and cold—"

"I'm all right," he insisted. "And you'll be right there, holding onto the rope I'll have tied about my waist. It won't take long—it's right at the edge there. I'll be all right long enough to see what's there."

Reluctantly she agreed, then questioned him as

they went back inside the cavern again.

"But I do not see why they would put even a chest in there," she said, and shivered, looking at the dark waters.

Jim indicated the shelf of rock overhead.

"My idea is that they had it in an iron chest, or box, and that they really put it back up there on the shelf," he said. "And when that earthquake came along and shook loose a chunk of the Giant, and slid it down to hide the opening and close the door, the same shake probably joggled the chest off into the creek. Being heavy, it didn't go far— maybe a piece of rock or something was above or below it, to help hold it in place. Anyway, I hit something down there, and that's my guess. We'll soon find out."

With the rope about his waist, he lowered himself into the water, stooping over, fumbling about. There it was—and then, with it in his arms, he strained to lift it. It was a chest, there was no doubt of that, and even in the water it was heavy.

Twenty-Two

Then, as he had it at the surface, he understood why it was so heavy. It was an iron chest—he had been right in that guess. And maybe it had been chosen to hide valuables in, a score or so of years before, as a proper strong box. It was a couple of feet long, by about a foot and a half wide and deep.

But apparently the catch, or lock, had not been too secure in the first place. Now the lid was back, the box was open—and apparently had been that way for a long time, perhaps years, there on the bottom of the underground stream. The box was full of water, which made up a lot of the weight.

He spilled most of the water out. There was something in the chest, but whether it was anything more than mud and sediment he could not tell. He set it on the rocky shore, climbed out after it. Already, he was shivering with the fresh bite of the cold.

Wordlessly, the rope still about his waist, he picked the chest up and carried it out into the sunshine, Jeanne beside him. The edge of the chest, and its opened lid, was rusty, corroded, rather sharp. He turned it upside down, and a small pile of stuff lay there. Something gleamed in the sun.

He picked it up and held it, and Jeanne's eyes grew big. So did his own. There was mud and slime about it, still to be washed off, but even now it was something to look at. A string of pearls— and the water had not harmed them, of course. They were lustrous, gleaming, and the string had not broken.

As the sun caught them, and Jeanne held them up, Jim caught his breath. Once or twice he had seen pearls, real pearls, and there was no question but that these were the real things, too. Perfectly matched, large, exquisite, with a soft, pink translucence shining through the milky whiteness of them—this was a string of pearls to adorn the bosom of a queen, or that of a harem favorite in a princely state of the Far East.

He took them and slipped them over Jeanne's

head. The string was long enough for him to do that without bothering with the clasp. He saw her eyes grow big and shining, luminous with the pearls.

"Oh, Jeem!" she breathed rapturously.

"Those are the real thing—fit for a queen," he said. "And they're yours, Jeanne! There was some treasure, anyhow."

That was not all. There was another necklece, unbroken—and these, rich and red and mignificent in the sun, could be nothing but rubies. Rubies as large as robin's eggs, red as blood. Here was a king's ranson, in those two articles alone.

Apparently that was all. Then he found one other thing—a ring, small, exquisite, of gold which the water had been helpless against, set with one large, flawless diamond. A woman's ring. He held it up, hesitated, then slipped it onto Jeanne's finger —the third finger of her left hand.

"It just fits!" she breathed.

"Know what a ring like that means?" he asked.

She looked at him, her eyes suddenly shy, looked as quickly away again, and nodded.

"Do—do you want me to wear it—Jeem?" she whispered.

"Of course," he agreed. "If—if you will!"

Suddenly she was in his arms, regardless of his wetness. Her arms clung to him.

"Now I am ver' happy, Jeem," she said. And again, he knew that here was the woman, to have and to hold—and a woman who knew what she wanted, just as he knew what he wanted.

"Is—is that all?" she asked presently, holding up the rubies, admiring the flash and beauty of them in the last of the westering sun.

"Seems to be," he said. "I have an idea that there was a lot more, to start with. Probably this chest was pretty well filled with stuff, like as not. But when the quake shook it down, it must have hit just right to break the lid open, and the current got away with the rest. Maybe there's a fortune, scattered along for the next few miles."

Jeanne shivered a little, thinking of that dark river. Then she smiled.

"But what does it matter?" she asked. "They did not belong to us, and we do not need them. We could not have found their owners, to geeve them back. And this—" She glanced at the ring on her finger, colored warmly, then fingered the pearls. "This is enough."

Jim felt the same way about it. They had found the treasure, and that was enough.

"You're forgetting these, aren't you?" he asked, holding up the rubies. "Gives you two of the finest necklaces any woman on earth ever had, you know."

This necklace was a little smaller. He had found the catch, and, though it was rather corroded and hard to work, he had it loose now, and he slipped that necklace, too, around her neck. Jeanne's eyes shone as she looked at them; then she took them off again.

"I was not forgetting, Jeem," she said. "These—they will be just right for Alice, with her red hair. She will love them."

He looked at her a little incredulously. He knew that the two girls were fast friends now, but such a gift was rather more than casual, to say the least.

"Do you have any idea how much those are worth?" he asked.

Jeanne nodded rather abstractedly.

"A lot of money—a great lot," she agreed. "But what does that matter? She will love them—and she has never had anything nice like that. And the pearls are just right for me, just as these are right for her." She fingered the pearls again. "They are all I want, Jeem—them—and this!" She glanced pridefully at the diamond.

They got their horses, turned back. The sun had set, and his clothes were still wet, but Jim had forgotten about being cold. He looked down at his own finger, at the silver cayuse rearing there, and then across to the other ring which he had given Jeanne. For since he had been the one to find the treasure, or the remnants of it, that ring had been his to give.

Jeanne met his glance, flushed warmly, and smiled.

"They are talking of getting married, Jeem," she said. "I heard them today."

"They?" He stared. "Who? Oh—you mean Bob and Alice?"

"But of course. Who else? They are ver' much in love."

"I was thinking of us," he said. "Did I tell you that I'm very much in love—with you, Jeanne?"

"No," she said gravely. "You did not. Yet I knew it. But I like to hear you say so, Jeem."

"You're going to hear me say it a lot," he agreed. "And how about you?"

"I theenk I have loved you from the time I first saw you, Jeem," she confessed. "Even when I—when I held that gun on you. But eet—it was not loaded," she added.

"Not loaded?" He laughed suddenly. "What a woman you are! Just the same, you shot me with it—playin' Cupid, I reckon. And so they're aimin' to get hitched, eh?" We might make it sort of a double affair, eh?"

Again she nodded, matter of factly.

"Of course," she said. "And I was thinking—this Ranch of the Giants, eet—it is a big one, with a lot of work to do. And Bob, he seems to be ver' good. Should we not give him the job of foreman, Jeem?"

"That's a right good idea," he agreed. "I was thinkin' the same thing myself. Give me more time for other things."

"You mean," she asked, her eyes dancing, "for to lie on your back in the sun, and to be lazy?"

"Sure," he conceded. "Plenty of that. That's the best sort of thing I do. And here in California, there's more sun than in some places—guess that's one reason I came out here in the first place. But what I was really thinkin' of—"

"Yes?" she asked, her horse now close to his as they ambled along.

"Give me more time for a proper sort of a honeymoon," he added. "That's somethin' that oughtn't to be rushed. I aim to stretch it out—to about fifty years, say. With a high point, halfway in between."

"Of course," Jeanne agreed. "But why halfway, Jeem?"

"That'll be our silver anniversary," he exclaimed. "And don't we owe it all to the luck of this silver cayuse, anyhow?"